KU-488-090

Contents

TO

GWEN

William—The Fourth

also published by
Macmillan Children's Books

Just—William
More William
William Again

©1979 Norman Thelwell

.thelwell.

this book belongs to

"YOU CAN LOOK AT THE ALBUM WHILE I AM GETTING READY."
WILLIAM WAS TRAPPED, TRAPPED IN A HUGE AND HORRIBLE
DRAWING-ROOM, BY A HUGE AND HORRIBLE WOMAN.

(*See page 31*)

Chapter 1

The Weak Spot

"You see," said Jameson Jameson, "we're all human beings. That's a very important point. You must admit that we're all human beings?"

Jameson Jameson, aged nineteen and three-quarters, was very eloquent. He paused more for rhetorical effect than because he really needed confirmation on the point. His audience, all under nineteen, agreed hoarsely and unanimously.

They were all human beings. They admitted it.

"Well, then," Jameson continued, warming to his subject, "as human beings we're equal. As being equal we've got equal rights, I suppose. Anyone deny that?"

Robert Brown, aged seventeen, in whose room the meeting took place, leaned forward eagerly. He was thoroughly enjoying the meeting. The only drawback was the presence of his younger brother, William, aged eleven. By some mistake someone had admitted William, and by some still greater mistake no one had ejected him; and now it was too late. He gave no excuse for ejection. He was sitting motionless, his hands on his knees, his eyes, under their untidy shock of hair, glued on the speaker, his mouth wide open. There was no doubt at all that he was impressed. But Robert wished he wasn't there. He felt that the presence of a kid was an insult to the mature intelligences round him, most of whom were in their first year at college.

But no one seemed to mind, so he contented himself with sitting so that he could not see William.

"Well," continued Jameson Jameson, "then why aren't we equal? Why are some rich and some poor? Why do some work and others not? Tell me that."

There was no answer—only a gasp of wonder and admiration.

Jameson Jameson (whose parents had perpetrated on him the supreme practical joke of giving him his surname for a Christian name, so that people who addressed him by his full name always seemed to be indulging in some witticism) brought down his fist upon the table with a bang.

"Then it's somebody's duty to make us equal. It's only common justice, isn't it? You admit that? Those who haven't any money must be given money, and those who have too much must have some taken off them. We want Equality. And no more Tyranny. The working-class must have Freedom. And who's going to do it?"

He thrust his hand into his coat front in a manner reminiscent of the late Mr. Gladstone and glared at his audience from under scowling brows.

"Ah, who?" gasped the audience.

"It's here that the Bolshevists come in!"

"Bolshevists?" said Robert, aghast.

"The Bolshevists are very much misjudged and—er—maligned," retorted Jameson Jameson, with emotion. "Shamefully misjudged and——" he wasn't sure whether he'd pronounced it right, so he ended feebly, "what I said before. I'm not," he admitted frankly, "in direct communication with Lenin, but I've read about it in a magazine, and I know a bit about it from that. The Bolshevists want to share things out so as we're equal, and that's only right, isn't it? 'Cause we're all human beings, and as such are equal, and as such have equal rights. Well, that's clear, isn't it? Does anyone," he glared round fiercely, "wish to contradict me?"

No one did. William, who was sitting in a draught, sneezed and was annihilated by a glance from Robert.

"Well," he continued, "I propose to form a Bolshevist Society, first of all, just to start with. You see, the Bolshevists have gone to extremes, but we'll join the Bolshevist party and—and purge it of all where it's wrong now. Now, who'll join the Society?"

As human beings with equal rights they were all anxious to join. They were all fired to the soul by Jameson Jameson's eloquence. Even William pressed onward to give in his name, but was sternly ordered away by Robert.

"But I believe all you do," he pleaded wistfully, "'bout want'n other people's money an' thinking we oughtn't to work."

"You've misunderstood me, my young friend," said Jameson Jameson, with a sigh, "but we want numbers. There's no reason why——"

"If that kid belongs, I'm not going to," said Robert firmly.

"We might have a Junior Branch——" suggested one of them.

So thus it was finally settled. William became the Junior Branch of the Society of Reformed Bolshevists. Alone he was President and Secretary and Committee and Members. He resented any suggestion of enlarging the Junior Branch. He preferred to form the Branch himself. He held meetings of his Branch under the laurel bushes in the garden, and made eloquent speeches to an audience consisting of a few depressed daffodil roots, and sometimes the cat from next door.

"All gotter be equal," he pronounced fiercely, "all gotter have lots of money. All 'uman beings. That's *sense*, isn't it? Is it *sense* or isn't it?"

The cat from next door scratched its ear and slowly winked.

"Well, *then*," said William, "someone ought to *do* somethin'."

The Society of Advanced Bolshevists met next month in Robert's room. William had left nothing to chance. He had heard Robert saying that he'd see no kids got in on this one, so he installed himself under Robert's bed before anyone arrived. Robert looked round the room with a keen and threatening gaze before he ushered Jameson Jameson into the chair, or, to be more accurate, on to the bed. The meeting began.

"Comrades," began Jameson Jameson, "we have, I hope, all spent this time in thinking things out and making ourselves more devoted to the cause. But now is the time for action. We've got to *do* something. If we had any money 'cept the mean bit that our fathers allow us we could make people jolly well sit up—we could——"

Here William, who had just inhaled a large mouthful of dust, sneezed loudly, and Robert made a dive beneath the bed. In the scuffle that ensued William embedded his teeth deeply into Jameson Jameson's ankle, and vengeance was vowed on either side.

"Well, why can't I come? I'm a Bolshevist too like wot all you are!"

"Well, you've got a Branch of your own," said Robert fiercely.

Jameson Jameson was still standing on one leg and holding the other in two hands with an expression of (fortunately) speechless agony on his face.

"Look!" went on Robert, "you may have maimed

WILLIAM MADE ELOQUENT SPEECHES TO AN AUDIENCE OF
DEPRESSED DAFFODIL ROOTS AND THE CAT FROM NEXT DOOR.

him for life for all you know, and he's the life and soul of
the Cause, and what can he do with a maimed foot?
You'll have to keep him all his life if he is maimed for
life, and when the Bolshevists get in power he'll have
your blood—and I shan't mind," he added, darkly.

Jameson Jameson gave a feeble smile.

"It's all right, Comrade," he said, "I harbour no
thoughts of vengeance. I hope I can bear more than this
for the Cause."

Very ungently William was deposited on the landing
outside.

"You can keep your nasty little Branch to yourself,
and don't come bothering us," was Robert's parting
shot.

It was then that William realised the power of
numbers. He resolved at once to enlarge his Branch.

Rubbing the side on which he had descended on the
landing, and frowning fiercely, he went downstairs and
out into the road. Near the gate was Victor Jameson,
Jameson Jameson's younger brother, gazing up at
Robert's bedroom window, which could be seen
through the trees.

"He's up there talkin'," he muttered scornfully.
"Doesn't he *talk*?"

The tone of contempt was oil on the troubled waters
of William's feelings.

"I've just bit him hard," he said modestly.

The two linked arms affectionately and set off down
the road. At the corner of the road they fell in with
George Bell. William had left Ronald Bell, George's
elder brother leaning against the mantelpiece in
Robert's room and examining himself in the glass. He
was letting his hair grow long, and he hoped it was
beginning to show.

"What do they *do* up at your house?" demanded

George with curiosity. "He won't tell me anything. He says it's secret. He says no one's got to know now, but all the world will know some day. That's what he *says*."

"*Huh*," said Victor scornfully. "They *talk*. That's all they do. They *talk*."

"Let's find a few more," said William, "an' I'll tell you all about it."

It being Saturday afternoon they soon collected the few more, and the company returned to the summer-house at the end of William's garden. The company consisted chiefly of younger brothers of the members of the gathering upstairs.

William rose to address them with one hand inside his coat in an attitude copied faithfully from Jameson Jameson.

"They gotter ole society," he said, "an' they've made me a Branch, so I can make all you Branches. So, now you're all Branches. See? Well, they say how we're all 'uman bein's an' equal. Well, they say if we're equal we oughtn't to have less money an' things than other folks, and more work to do, an' all that. That's wot I heard 'em say."

Here the cat from next door, drawn by the familiar sound of William's voice, peered into the summerhouse, and was promptly dismissed by a well-aimed stick. It looked reproachfully at William as it departed.

"And to-day they said," went on William, "that now is the time for *Action*, an' how we'd only the mean bit of money our fathers gave us; and then they found me an' I bit his leg, and they threw me out, an' I bet I've got a big ole bruise on my side, an' I bet he's got a bigger ole bite on his leg."

He sat down, amid applause, and George, acting with a generosity born of a sudden feeling of comradeship, took a stick of rock from his pocket and passed it round

for a suck each. This somewhat disturbed the harmony
of the meeting, as "Ginger," William's oldest friend,
was accused of biting a piece off, and the explanation,
that it "came off in his mouth," was not accepted by the
irate owner, who was already regretting his generosity.
The combatants were parted by William, and peace was
sealed by the passing round of a bottle of liquorice water
belonging to Victor Jameson.

Then William rose for a second speech.

"Well, we're all Branches, so let's do same as them.
They're goin' to get equal cause they're 'uman bein's; so
let's try and get equal too."

"Equal with what?" demanded Douglas, whose elder
brother had joined Jameson Jameson's society, and had
secretly purchased a red tie, which he did not dare to
wear in public, but which he donned behind a tree on his
way to William's house, and doffed in the same place on
his way from William's house.

"Equal to *them*," said William. "Why, just think of
the things they've got. They've got lots of money,
haven't they?—lots more than what we have, an' they
can buy anything they want, an' they stay up for dinner
always, and go out late at night, an' eat what they want
with no one sayin' had they better, or cert'nly not, or
what happened last time, an' they smoke an' don't go to
school, an' go to the pictures, an' they've got lots more
things 'n we've got—bicycles an' grammerphones, an'
fountain-pens, an' watches, an' things what we've not
got. Well, an' we're 'uman beings, too, an' we ought to
be equal, an' why shun't we be equal?—an' now's the
time for *Action!* They said so."

There was a silence.

"But——" said Douglas slowly, "we can't just *take*
things, can we?"

"Yes," said William, "we *can* if we're Bolshevists.

"... AN' WE'RE 'UMAN BEINGS, TOO, AN' WE OUGHT TO BE
EQUAL, AN' WHY SHUN'T WE BE EQUAL? ..."

They said so. An' we're all Bolshevist Branches. They
made me, an' I made you. See? So we can take anything
to make us equal. See? We've got to be equal."

Here the meeting was stopped by the spectacle of the
Senior Bolshevists issuing from the side door wearing
frowns of stern determination. Douglas's brother
fingered his red tie ostentatiously; Ronald pulled down
his cap over his eyes with the air of a conspirator;
Jameson Jameson limped slightly and smiled patiently
and forgivingly upon Robert, who was still apologising
for William. The words that were wafted across to
listening ears upon the Spring breeze were: "Next
Tuesday, then."

Then the Branches turned to a discussion of details.
They were nothing if not practical. After about a quarter

of an hour they departed, each pulling his cap over his eye and frowning. As they departed they murmured: "Next Tuesday, then."

Next Tuesday dawned bright and clear, with no hint that it was one of those days on which the world's fate is decided.

The Senior Bolshevists met in the morning. They discussed the possibility of getting into touch with Lenin, but no one knew his exact address, or the rate of postage to Russia, so no definite step was taken.

During the afternoon Robert followed his father into the library. His face was set and stern.

"Look here, father," he said, "we've been thinking— some of us. Things don't seem fair. We're all human beings. It's time for action. We've all agreed to speak to our fathers to-day and point things out to them. They've been misjudged and maligned, but we're going to purge them of all that. You see, we're all human beings, and it's time for action. We're all agreed on that. We've got equal rights, because we're all human beings."

He paused, inserted a finger between his neck and collar as if he found its pressure intolerable, then smoothed back his hair. He was looking almost apoplectic.

"I don't know whether I make my meaning clear," he began again.

"You don't, old chap, whatever it may be," said his father soothingly. "Perhaps you feel the heat?—or the Spring? You ought to take something cooling, and then lie down for a few hours."

"You don't understand," said Robert desperately. "It's life or death to civilisation. You see, we're all human beings, and all equal, and we've got equal rights, and yet some have all the things, and some have none. You see, we thought we'd all start at home and get things

made more fair there, and our fathers to divide up the
money more fairly and give us our real share, and then
we could go round teaching other people to give things
up to other people and share things out more fairly. You
see, we must begin at home, and then we start fair.
We're all human beings with equal rights."

"You're so very modest in your demands," said
Robert's father. "Would half be enough for you? Are
you sure you wouldn't like a little more?"

Robert waved the suggestion aside.

"No," he said, "you see, you have the others to keep.
But we've all decided to ask our fathers to-day, then we
can start fair and have some funds to go on. A society
without funds seems to be so handicapped. And it would
be an example to other fathers all over the world. You
see——"

At this moment Robert's mother came in.

"What a mess your room's in, Robert! I hope William
hasn't been rummaging in it."

Robert turned pale.

"William!" he gasped, and fled to investigate.

He returned in a few minutes, almost inarticulate with
fury.

"My watch!" he said. "My purse! Both gone! I'm
going after him."

He seized his hat from the hall, and started to the
door. His father watched him, leaning easily against the
doorpost of the library, and smiling.

From the garden as he passed came a wail.

"My bicycle! Gone too. The shed's empty!"

In the road he met Jameson Jameson.

"Burglars!" said Jameson Jameson. "All my money's
been taken. And my camera! The wretches! I'm going to
scour the country for them."

Various other members of the Bolshevist Society

appeared, filled with wrath and lamenting vanished treasures.

"It can't be burglars," said Robert, "because why only us?"

"Do you think someone in the Government found out about us being Bolshevists and is trying to intimidate us?"

Jameson Jameson thought this very likely, and they discussed it excitedly in the middle of the road, some hatless, some hatted, all talking breathlessly. Then at the other end of the road appeared a group of boys. They were happy, rollicking boys. They all carried bags of sweets which they ate lavishly and handed round to their friends equally lavishly. One held a camera—or the remains of a camera—whose mechanism the entire party had just been investigating. One more had a large wrist-watch upon a small wrist. One walked (or rather leapt) upon a silver-topped walking-stick. One, the quietest of the group, was smoking a cigarette. At the side near the ditch about half a dozen rode intermittently upon a bicycle. The descent of the bicycle and its cargo into the ditch was greeted with roars of laughter. They were very happy boys. They sang as they walked.

"We've been to the pictures."

"In the best seats."

"Bought lots of sweets and a mouth-organ."

"We've got a bicycle, an' a camera, an' two watches, an' a fountain-pen, an' a razor, an' a football, an' lots of things."

White with fury, the Senior Bolshevists charged down upon them. The Junior Bolshevists stood their ground firmly, with the exception of the one who had been smoking a cigarette, and he, perforce a coward for physical rather than moral reasons, crept quietly home, relinquishing without reluctance his half-smoked

THEN AT THE OTHER END OF THE ROAD APPEARED A GROUP OF
BOYS. THEY WERE HAPPY, ROLLICKING BOYS.

cigarette. In the Homeric battle that followed, accusa-
tions and justifications were hurled to and fro as the
struggle proceeded.

"You beastly little thieves!"

"You said to be equal, an' why should some people
have all the things!"

"You little wretches!"

"We're 'uman beings an' got to *take* things to make
equal. You *said* so."

"Give it back to me!"

"Why should you have it an' not me? It was time for
Action, you said."

"You've *spoilt* it."

"Well, it's as much mine as yours. We've got equal rights. We're all 'uman beings."

But the battle was one-sided, and the Junior Branch, having surrendered their booty and received punishment, fled in confusion. The Senior Branch, bending lovingly and sadly over battered treasures, walked slowly and silently up the road.

*   *   *

"About your Society——" began Mr. Brown after dinner.

"No," said Robert, "it's all off. We've given it up, after all. We don't think there's much in it, after all. None of us do, now. We feel quite different."

"But you were so enthusiastic about it this afternoon. Sharing fairly, and all that sort of thing."

"Yes," said Robert. "That's all very well, It's all right when you can get your share of other people's things, but when other people try to get their share of your things, then it's different."

"Ah," said Mr. Brown, "that's the weak spot. I'm glad you found it out."

Chapter 2

William and Photography

Mrs. Adolphus Crane was William's mother's second cousin and William's godmother. Among the many senseless institutions of grown-up life the institutions of godmothers and godfathers seemed to William the most senseless of all. Moreover, Mrs. Adolphus Crane was rich and immensely respectable—the last person whom Fate should have selected as his godmother. Fortunately, she lived at a distance, and so was spared the horrible spectacle of William's daily crimes. His meetings with her had not been fortunate, so far, in spite of his family's earnest desire that he should impress her favourably.

There had been that terrible meeting two months ago. William was running a race with one of his friends. It was quite a novel race invented by William. The competitors each had their mouths full of water and the one who could run the farthest without either swallowing his load or discharging it, won. William in the course of the race encountered Mrs. Adolphus Crane, who was on her way to William's house to pay him a surprise visit. She recognised him and addressed to him a kindly, affectionate remark. Of course, if he had had time to think over the matter from all points of view, he might have conceived the idea of swallowing the water before he answered. But, as he afterwards explained, he had no time to think. The worst of it was that the painful incident was witnessed by almost all William's family from the drawing-room window. Mrs. Adolphus Crane's visit on that occasion was a very short one. She seemed slightly distant. It was felt strongly that something must be done to win back her favour. William disclaimed all responsibility.

"Well, I can't help it. I *can't* help it. I don't mind. Honestly I don't mind if she doesn't like me. Well, I don't mind if she doesn't come again, either."

"But, William, she's your godmother."

"Well," said the goaded William. "I can't help *that*. I didn't do *that*."

When Mrs. Adolphus Crane's birthday came, William's mother attacked him again.

"You ought to give her something William, you know, especially after the way you treated her the last time she came over."

"I've nothin' to give her," said William simply. "She can have that book Uncle George gave me, if she likes. Yes, she can have that." He warmed to the subject. "You know. The one about Ancient Hist'ry. I don't mind her having it a bit."

"But you haven't read it."

"I don't mind not readin' it," said William generously. "I—I'd like her to have it," he went on.

But it was Mrs. Brown who had the great inspiration.

"We'll have William's photograph taken for her."

It was quite simple to say that, and it was quite simple to make an appointment at the photographer's, but it was another matter to provide an escort for him. Mrs. Brown happened to have a bad cold; Mr. Brown was at the office; Robert, William's grown-up brother, flatly refused to go with him. So, after a conversation that lasted almost an hour, William's elder sister Ethel was induced, mainly by bribery and corruption, to go with

William to the photographer's. But she took a friend with her to act as a buffer state.

William, at the appointed hour, was in a state of suppressed fury. To William the lowest depth of humiliation was having his photograph taken. Mrs. Brown had expended much honest toil upon him. He had been washed and brushed and combed and manicured till his spirits had sunk below zero. To William, complete cleanliness was quite incompatible with happiness. He had been encased in his "best suit"—a thing of hard, unbending cloth; with that horror of horrors, a stiff collar.

"Won't a jersey do?" he had asked plaintively. "It'll probably make me ill—give me a sore throat or somethin'—this tight thing at my neck, an' I wouldn't like to be ill—'cause of giving you trouble," he ended piously.

Mrs. Brown was touched—she was the one being in the world who never lost faith in William.

"But you wear it every Sunday, dear," she protested.

"Sundays is different," he said. "Everyone wears silly things on Sundays—but, but s'pose I met someone on my way there." His horror was pathetic.

"Well, you look very nice, dear. Where are your gloves."

"*Gloves?*" he said indignantly.

"Yes—to keep your hands clean till you get there."

"Is anyone goin' to *give* me anythin' for doin' all this?"

She sighed.

"No, dear. It's to give pleasure to your godmother. I know you like to give people pleasure." William was silent, cogitating over this entirely new aspect of his character.

He set off down the road with Ethel and her friend

Blanche. Bosom friends of his, with jerseys, with normal dirty hands and faces, passed him and stared at him in amazement.

He acknowledged their presence only by a cold stare. On ordinary days he was a familiar figure on that road himself, also comfortably jerseyed and gloriously dirty. He would then have greeted them with a war-whoop and a friendly punch. But now he was an outcast, a pariah, a thing apart—a boy in his best clothes and kid gloves on an ordinary morning.

The photographer was awaiting them. William returned his smile of welcome with a scowl.

"So this is our little friend?" said the photographer. "And what is his name?"

William grew purple.

Ethel began to enjoy it.

"Willie," she said.

Now, there were many insults that William had learned to endure with outward equanimity, but this was not one. Ethel knew perfectly well his feeling with regard to the name "Willie". It was a deliberate revenge because she had to waste a whole morning on him. Moreover, Ethel had various scores to wipe off against William, and it was not often that she had him entirely at her mercy.

William growled. That is the only word that describes the sound emitted.

"Pretty name for a pretty boy," commented the photographer in sprightly vein.

Ethel and Blanche gurgled. William, dark and scowling, looked unspeakable things at them.

"Come forward," said the photographer invitingly. "Any preparations? Fancy dress?"

"I think not," gurgled Ethel.

"I have some nice costumes," he persisted. "A little

page? Bubbles? But perhaps the hair is hardly suitable. Cupid? I have some pretty wings and drapery. But perhaps the little boy's expression is hardly—— No, I think not," hastily, as he encountered the fixed intensity of William's scowling gaze. "Remove the cap and gloves, my little chap."

He looked up and down William's shining, immaculate person. "Ah, very nice."

He waved Ethel and Blanche to a seat.

"Now, my boy——"

He waved the infuriated William to a rustic woodland scene at the other end.

"Now, stand just here. That's right. No, not quite so stiff—and—no, not quite so hunched up, my little chap . . . the hands resting carelessly . . . one on the hip, I think . . . just easy and natural . . . *that's* right . . . but no, hardly. Relax the brow a little. And—ah, no . . . not a grimace . . . it would spoil a pretty picture . . . the feet *so* . . . and the head *so* . . . the hair is slightly deranged . . . that's better."

Let it stand to William's eternal credit that he resisted the temptation to bite the photographer's hand as it strayed among his short locks. At last he was posed and the photographer returned to the camera, but during his return William moved feet, hands, and head to an easier position. The photographer sighed.

"Ah, he's moved. William's moved. What a pity! We'll have to begin all over again."

He returned to William, and very patiently he rearranged William's feet and hands and head.

"The toes turned out—not in, you see, Willie, and the hands *so*, and the head slightly on one side . . . *so*, no, not right down on to the shoulder . . . ah, that's right . . . that's sweet, a very pretty picture."

Ethel had retired hysterically behind a screen.

The photographer returned to his camera. William promptly composed his limbs more comfortably.

"Ah, what a pity! Willie's moved again. We shall have to commence afresh."

He returned to William and again put his unwilling head on one side, his hand upon his hip, and turned William's stout boots at a graceful angle.

He returned. William was clinging doggedly to his pose. Anything to put an end to this torture.

"Ah, right," commented the photographer. "Splendid! Ve-ery pretty. The head just a lee-eetle more on one side. The expression a lee-eetle less—melancholy. A smile, please—just a lee-eetle smile. Ah, no," hastily, as William savagely bared his teeth, "perhaps it is better without the smile." Suppressed gurgles came from behind the screen where Ethel clung helplessly to Blanche. "One more, please. *Sitting*, I think, this time. The legs crossed—easily and naturally—*so*. The elbow resting on the arm of the chair and the cheek upon the hand—*so*." He retired to a distance and examined the effect, with his head on one side. "A little spoilt by the expression, perhaps—but very pretty. The expression a lee-eetle less—er—fierce, if you will pardon the word." William here deigned to speak.

"I can't look any different to this," he remarked coldly.

"Now, think of the things I say," went on the photographer, brightly. "Sweeties? Ah!" looking merrily at William's unchanging ferocious expression. "Do I see a saucy little smile?" As a matter of fact, he didn't, because at that moment Ethel, her eyes streaming, peeped round the screen for another look at the priceless sight of William in his best suit, in the familiar attitude of the Bard of Avon. Encountering the concentrated fury of William's gaze, she retired hastily.

AT THAT MOMENT ETHEL PEEPED ROUND THE SCREEN FOR
ANOTHER LOOK AT THE PRICELESS SIGHT OF WILLIAM IN THE
FAMILIAR ATTITUDE OF THE BARD OF AVON.

"Seaside with spade and bucket?" went on the
photographer, watching William's unchanging expression. "Pantomimes? That nice, soft, furry pussy cat
you've got at home?" But seeing William's expression
change from one of scornful fury to one of Nebuchad-
nezzan rage and fury, he hastily pressed the little ball lest
worse should follow.

Ethel's description of the morning considerably
enlivened the lunch table. Only Mrs. Brown did not join
in the roars of laughter.

"But I think it sounds very nice, dear," she said, "very
nice. I'm very much looking forward to the proofs
coming."

"Well, it was priceless," said Ethel. "It was ever so
much funnier than the pantomime. I wouldn't have
missed it for anything. For years to come, if I feel

depressed, I shall just think of William this morning. His face . . . oh, his face!''

William defended himself.

"My face is jus' like anyone else's face," he said indignantly. "I don't know why you're all laughing. There's nothin' funny about my face. I've never *done* anythin' to it. It's no different to other people's. It doesn't make *me* laugh."

"No, dear," said Mrs. Brown soothingly, "it's very nice—very nice, indeed. And I'm sure it will be a beautiful photograph."

The proofs arrived the next week. They were highly appreciated by William's family. There were two positions. In one, William in an attitude of intellectual contemplation, glowered at them from an artistic background; in the other, he stood stiffly with one hand on his hip, his toes (in spite of all) turned resolutely in, and glared ferociously and defiantly upon the world in general. Mrs. Brown was delighted. "I think it's awfully nice," she said, "and he looks so smart and clean."

William, mystified by Robert's and Ethel's reception of them, carried them up to his room and studied them long and earnestly.

"Well, I can't see wot's *funny* about them," he said at last, half indignantly and half mystified. "It doesn't seem funny to *me*."

"You'll have to write a letter to your godmother, dear," said Mrs. Brown, as Mrs. Adolphus Crane's birthday drew near.

"*Me?*" said William bitterly. "I should think I've done *enough* for her."

"No," said Mrs. Brown firmly, "you *must* write a letter."

"I dunno what to say to her."

"Say whatever comes into your head."

"I dunno how to *spell* all the words that come in my head."

"I'll help you, dear."

Seeing no escape, William sat gloomily down at the table and was supplied with pen, ink, and paper. He looked round disapprovingly.

"S'pose I wear out the nib?" he said sadly. Mrs. Brown obligingly placed a box of nibs at his elbow. He sighed wearily. Life sometimes is hardly worth living.

After much patient thought he got as far as "Dear Godmother." He occupied the next ten minutes in seeing how far you could bend apart the two halves of a nib without breaking them. After breaking six, he wearied of the occupation and returned to his letter. With deeply-furrowed brow and protruding tongue he continued his efforts. "Many happy returns of your birthday. I hopp you are verry well. I am very well and so is mother and father and Ethel and Robbert." He gazed out of the window and chewed the end of his penholder into splinters. Some he swallowed, then choked, and had to retire for a drink of water. Then he demanded a fresh pen. After about fifteen minutes he returned to his epistolary efforts.

"It is not raning to-day," he wrote, after much thought. Then, "It did not rane yesterday and we are hoppin' it will not rane to-morrow."

Having exhausted that topic, he scratched his head in despair, wrinkled up his brows, and chewed his penholder again.

"I have a hole in my stokking," was his next effort. Then, "I have had my phottograf took and send it for a birthday present. Some people think it funny but to me it seems alrite. I hopp you will like it. Your loving godsun, William."

Mrs. Adolphus Crane was touched, both by letter and photograph.

"I must have been wrong," she said with penitence. "He looks so *good*. And there's something rather *sad* about his face."

She asked William to her birthday tea-party. To William this was the climax of a long chain of insults.

"But I don't *want* to go to tea with her," he said in dismay.

"But she wants you, darling," said Mrs. Brown. "I expect she liked your photograph."

"I'm not going," said William testily, "if they're all going to be laughing at my photograph all the time. I'm jus' sick of people laughing at my photograph."

"Of course they won't, dear," said Mrs. Brown. "It's a very nice photograph. You look a bit—depressed in it, that's all."

"Well, that's not *funny*," he said indignantly.

"Of course not, dear. You'll behave nicely, won't you?"

"I'll behave ordinary," he said coldly, "but I don't want to go. I don't want to go 'cause—'cause—' cause——" he sought silently for a reason that might appeal to a grown-up mind, then, with a brilliant inspiration, "'cause I don't want my best clothes to get all wore out."

"I don't think they will, dear," she said; "don't worry about that."

William dejectedly promised not to.

The afternoon of Mrs. Adolphus Crane's birthday dawned bright and clear, and William, resigned and martyred, set off. He arrived early and was shown into Mrs. Adolphus Crane's magnificent drawing-room. An air of magisterial magnificence shed gloom over Mrs. Adolphus Crane's whole house. Mrs. Adolphus Crane, as magisterial, and magnificent and depressing and enormous as her house, entered.

"Good afternoon, William. Now I've a pleasant little surprise for you." William's gloomy countenance brightened. "I've put your photograph into my album. There! What an honour for a little boy!" William's countenance relapsed into gloom.

"You can look at the album while I'm getting ready, and then when the guests come you can show it to them. Won't that be nice?" She departed.

William was trapped—trapped in a huge and horrible drawing-room by a huge and horrible woman, and he would have to stay there at least two hours. And Ginger and Henry were bird-nesting! Oh, the horror of it. Why was he chosen by Fate for this penance? He felt a sudden fury against the art of photography in general. William's sudden furies against anything demanded some immediate outlet.

So William, with the aid of a pencil, looked at Mrs. Adolphus Crane's family album till Mrs. Adolphus Crane was ready. Then she arrived, and soon after her the guests, or rather such of them as had not had the presence of mind to invent excuses for their absence. For, funeral affairs were Mrs. Adolphus Crane's parties. Liveliness and hilarity dropped slain on the doorstep. The guests came sadly into the drawing-room, and Mrs. Adolphus Crane dispensed gloom from the hearthrug. Her voice was low and deep.

"How do you do . . . thank you so much . . . I doubt whether I shall live to see another . . . yes, my nerves! By the way—my little godson——" They turned to look at William who was sitting in silent misery in a corner, his hands on his knees. He returned their interested stares with his best company frown. On the chair by him was the album. "Have you seen the family album?"

went on Mrs. Adolphus Crane. "It's most interesting. Do look at it." A group of visitors sadly gathered round it and one of them opened it. Mrs. Adolphus Crane did not join them. She knew her album by heart. She took her knitting, sat down by the fire, and poured forth her knowledge.

"The first one is great uncle Joshua," she said, "a splendid old man. Never touched tobacco or alcoholic drinks in his life."

They looked at great uncle Joshua. He sat, grim and earnest and respectable, with his hand on the table. But a lately-added pipe, in pencil, adorned his mouth, and his hand seemed to encircle a tankard. Quite suddenly animation returned to the group by the album. They began to believe that they were going to enjoy it, after all.

"Then comes my poor, dear mother." Poor, dear mother wore a large eye-glass with a black ribbon and a wild Indian head-dress. The group by the album grew large. There seemed to be some magnetic attraction about it.

"Then comes my paternal uncle James, a very handsome man."

Paternal uncle James might have been a very handsome man before his nose had been elongated for several inches, and his lips curved into an enormous smile, showing gigantic teeth. He smoked a large, vulgar-looking pipe.

"A beautiful character, too," said Mrs. Adolphus Crane. She continued the family catalogue, and the visitors followed the photographs in the album. They were all embellished. Some had pipes, some had blue noses, some black eyes, some giant spectacles, some comic head-dresses. Some had received more attention than others. Aunt Julia, "a most saintly woman," positively leered from her "cabinet," with a huge nose, and a black eye, and a cigar in her mouth. The album was handed from one to another. An unwonted hilarity and vivacity reigned supreme—and always there were crowds round the album.

Mrs. Adolphus Crane was surprised, but vaguely flattered. Her party seemed more successful than usual. People seemed to be taking quite a lot of notice of William, too. One young curate, who had wept tears over the album, pressed half a crown into William's hand. By some unerring instinct they guessed the author of the outrage. As a matter of fact, Mrs. Adolphus Crane did not happen to look at her album till several months later, and then it did not occur to her to connect it with William. But this afternoon she somehow connected the strange spirit of cheerfulness that pervaded her drawing-room with him, and was most gracious to him.

"He's been *so* good," she said to Mrs. Brown when she arrived to take William home; "quite helped to make my little party a success."

Mrs. Brown concealed her amazement as best she could.

"But what did you *do*, William?" she said on the way home as William plodded along beside her, his hands in his pockets lovingly fingering his half-crown.

"Me?" said William innocently. "Nothin'."

Chapter 3

The Fête—and Fortune

William took a fancy to Miss Tabitha Croft as soon as he saw her. She was small and inoffensive-looking. She didn't look the sort of person to write irate letters to William's parents. William was a great judge of character. He could tell at a glance who was likely to object to him, who was likely to ignore him, and who was likely definitely to encourage him. The last was a very rare class indeed. Most people belonged to the first class. But as he sat on the wall and watched Miss Tabitha Croft timidly and flutteringly superintending the unloading of her furniture at her little cottage gate, he came to the conclusion that she would be very inoffensive indeed. He also came to the conclusion that he was going to like her. William generally got on well with timid people. He was not timid himself. He was small and freckled and solemn and possessed of great tenacity of purpose for his eleven years.

Miss Tabitha, happening to look up from the débris of a small table which one of the removers had carelessly and gracefully crushed against the wall, saw a boy perched on her wall, scowling at her. She did not know that the scowl was William's ordinary normal expression. She smiled apologetically.

"Good afternoon," she said.

"Arternoon," said William.

There was silence for a time while another of the
removers took the door off its hinges with little or no
effort by means of a small piano which he then placed
firmly upon another remover's foot. Then the silence
was broken. During the breaking of silence, William's
scowl disappeared and a rapt smile appeared on his face.

"Can't they think of things to *say?*" he said delightedly to Miss Tabitha when a partial peace was restored.

Miss Tabitha raised a face of horror and misery.

"Oh, dear!" she said in a voice that trembled, "it's
simply dreadful!"

William's chivalry (that curious quality) was aroused.
He leapt heavily from the wall.

"I'll help," he said airily. "Don't you worry."

He helped.

He staggered from the van to the house and from the
house to the van. He worked till the perspiration poured
from his freckled brow. He broke two candlesticks, a
fender, a lamp, a statuette, and most of a breakfast
service. After each breakage he said, "Never mind,"
comfortingly to Miss Tabitha and put the pieces tidily in
the dustbin. When he had filled the dustbin he arranged
them in a neat pile by the side of it. He was completely
master of the situation. Miss Tabitha gave up the
struggle and sat on a packing-case in the kitchen with
some sal-volatile and smelling-salts. One of the removers gave William a drink of cold tea—another gave him a
bit of cold sausage. William was blissfully, riotously
happy. The afternoon seemed to fly on wings. He tore a
large hole in his knickers and upset a tin of paint, which
he found on a window sill, down his jersey. At last the
removers departed and William proudly surveyed the
scene of his labours and destruction.

"Well," he said, "I bet things would have been a lot
different if I hadn't helped."

"I'm sure they would," said Miss Tabitha with perfect truth.

"Seems about tea time, doesn't it?" went on William gently.

Miss Tabitha gave a start and put aside the sal-volatile.

"Yes; *do* stay and have some here."

"Thanks," said William simply, "I was thinking you'd most likely ask me."

Over the tea (to which he did full justice in spite of his previous repast of cold tea and sausage) William waxed very conversational. He told her of his friends and enemies (chiefly enemies) in the neighbourhood—of Farmer Jones who made such a fuss over his old apples, of the Rev. P. Craig who entered into a base conspiracy with parents to deprive quite well-meaning boys of their Sunday afternoon freedom. "If Sunday school's so *nice* an' *good for folks* as they say it is," said William bitterly, "why don't *they* go? I wun't mind *them* going."

He told her of Ginger's air-gun and his own catapult, of the dead rat they found in the ditch and the house they had made of branches in the wood, of the dare-devil career of robber and outlaw he meant to pursue as soon as he left school. In short, he admitted her unreservedly into his friendship.

And while he talked, he consumed large quantities of bread and jam and butter and cakes and pastry. At last he rose.

"Well," he said, "I s'pose I'd better be goin'."

Miss Tabitha was bewildered but vaguely cheered by him.

"You must come again . . ." she said.

"Oh, yes," said William cheerfully. "I'll come again lots . . . an' let me know when you're moving again—I'll come an' help again."

Miss Tabitha shuddered slightly.

"Thank you *so* much," she said.

*   *   *

He arrived the next afternoon.

"I've just come to see," he said, "how you're gettin' on."

Miss Tabitha was seated at a little table—with a row of playing cards spread out in front of her.

She flushed slightly.

"I'm—I'm just telling my fortune, William," she said.

"Oh," said William. He was impressed.

"It *does* sometimes come true," she said eagerly, "I do it nearly every day. It's curious—how it grows on one."

She began to turn up the covered cards and study them intently. William sat on a chair opposite her and watched with interest.

"There was a letter in my cards yesterday," she said, "and it came this morning. Sometimes it comes true like that, but often," she sighed, "it doesn't."

"Wot's in it to-day?" said William, scowling at the cards.

"A death," said Miss Tabitha in a sepulchral whisper, "and a letter from a dark man and jealousy of a fair woman and a present from across the sea and legal business and a legacy—but they're none of them the sort of thing that comes true. I don't know though," she went on dreamily, "the Income Tax man might be dark—I don't know—and I may hear from him soon. It's wonderful really—I mean that any of it should come out. It's quite an absorbing pursuit. Shall I do yours?"

"'Um," said William graciously.

"You must wish first."

William wished with his eyes screwed up in silent concentration.

"I've done it," he said.

Miss Tabitha dealt out the cards. She shook her head sorrowfully.

"You'll be treated badly by a fair woman," she said.

William agreed gloomily.

"That'll be Ethel—my sister," he said. "She thinks that jus' cause she's grown up . . ." He relapsed into subterranean mutterings.

"And you'll have your wish," she said.

William brightened. Then his eye roved round the room to a photograph on a bureau by the window.

"Who's he?" he said.

Miss Tabitha flushed again.

"He was once going to marry me," she said. "And he went away and he never came back."

"'Speck he met someone he liked better an' married her," suggested William cheerfully.

"I expect he did," said Miss Tabitha.

He surveyed her critically.

"Perhaps he didn't like your hair not being curly," he proceeded. "Some don't. My brother Robert he says if a girl's hair doesn't curl she oughter curl it. P'raps you didn't curl it."

"No, I didn't."

"My sister Ethel does, but she gets mad if I tell folks, an' she gets mad when I use her old things for makin' holes in apples and cardboard an' things. She's an awful fuss," he ended contemptuously.

When he got home he stood transfixed on the dining-room threshold, his mouth open, his eyes wide.

"Crumbs!" he ejaculated.

He had wished that there might be ginger cake for tea. And there was.

"YOU'LL BE TREATED BADLY BY A FAIR WOMAN," SHE SAID.
WILLIAM AGREED GLOOMILY. "THAT'LL BE ETHEL," HE SAID.

At tea was the Vicar's wife. The Vicar's wife was
afflicted with the Sale of Work mania. It is a disease to
which Vicars' wives are notoriously susceptible. She was
always thinking out the next but one Sale of Work
before the next one was over. She was always praised in
the local press and she felt herself to be a very happy
woman.

"I'm going to call the next one a Fête," she said. "It
will seem more of a change."

"Fake?" said William with interest.

She murmured "Dear boy," vaguely.

"We'll advertise it widely. I'm thinking of calling it the
King of Fêtes. Such an *arresting* title. We'll have donkey

rides and coconut shies, so *democratic*—and we ought to have fortune-telling. One doesn't—h'm—of course, *believe* in it—but it's what people expect. Some quite *harmless* fortune-telling—by cards, for instance——"

William gasped.

"She did mine—*wonderful*," he said excitedly, "it came—just wot I wished. There was it for tea!"

"Who? What?" said the Vicar's wife.

"The new one—at the cottage—I did all her furniture for her an' got paint on my clothes an' she told me about him not coming back 'cause of her hair p'raps an' I got some of her things broke but not many an' she gave me tea an' said to come again."

Gradually they elicited details.

"I'll call," said the Vicar's wife. "It would be so nice to have someone one *knows* to do it—someone *respectable*. Fortune-tellers are so often not *quite*—you know what I mean, dear," she cooed to William's mother.

"Of course," murmured William abstractedly, "it mayn't have been her hair. It may have been jus' anything. . . ."

*　　　*　　　*

William was having a strenuous time. Fate was making one of her periodic assaults on him. Everything went wrong. Miss Drew, his form mistress at school, had taken an altogether misguided and unsympathetic view of his zeal for nature study. In fact, when the beetle which William happened to be holding lovingly in his hand as he did his sums by her desk, escaped and made its way down her neck, her piercing scream boded no good to William. The further discovery of a caterpillar and two woodlice in his pencil-box, a frog in his satchel, and earwigs in his pocket, annoyed her still more, and William stayed in school behind his friends to write out one hundred times, "I must not bring insects into school." His addition "because they friten Miss Drew," made relations still more strained. He met with no better luck at home. His unmelodious and penetrating practices on a mouth-organ in the early hours of the morning had given rise to a coldness that changed to actual hostility when it was discovered that he had used Ethel's new cape as the roof of his wigwam in the garden and Robert's new expensive brown shoe polish to transform himself to a Red Indian chief. He was distinctly unpopular at home. There was some talk of not allowing him to attend the King of Fêtes, but as the rest of the family were going and the maids had refused to be left with William on the premises it was considered safer to allow him to go.

"But any of your *tricks*——" said his father darkly, leaving the sentence unfinished.

The day of the King of Fêtes was fine. The stalls were bedecked in the usual bright and inharmonious colours. A few donkeys with their attendants surveyed the scene contemptuously. Ethel was wearing the new cape (brushed and cleaned to a running accompaniment of abuse of William), Mrs. Brown was presiding at a stall. Robert, wearing a large buttonhole, with his shoes well browned (with a new tin of polish purchased with William's pocket-money) presided at a miniature rifle range. William, having been given permission to attend, and money for his entrance, hung round the gateway glaring at them scornfully. He always disliked his family intensely upon public occasions. He had not yet paid his money and was wondering whether it was worth it after all, and would it not be wiser to spend it on bulls' eyes and gingerbreads, and his afternoon in the fields as a solitary outlaw and hunter of cats or whatever other live prey Fate chose to send him. In a tent at the farther end of the Fête ground was Miss Tabitha Croft, arrayed in a long and voluminous garment covered with strange signs. They were supposed to be mystic Eastern signs, but were in reality the invention of the Vicar's wife, suggested by the freehand drawing of her youngest son, aged three. It completely enveloped Miss Tabitha from head to foot, leaving only two holes for her eyes and two holes for her arms. She had shown it to William the day before.

"I don't *quite* like it," she had confessed. "I hope there's nothing—blasphemous about it. But she ought to know—being a Vicar's wife she ought to know. I only hope," she went on, shaking her head, "that I'm not tampering with the powers of darkness—even for the cause of the church organ."

Outside was a large placard: "Fortune Telling by the Woman of Mystery, 2s. 6d. each." Inside the Woman of Mystery sat trembling with nervousness in front of a table on which reposed her little well-worn pack of cards, each with a neat hieroglyphic in the corner to show whether it meant a death or a wedding or a legacy or anything else.

William, surveying this scene from the gateway, became aware of a figure coming slowly down the road. It was a man—a very tall man who stooped slightly as he walked. As he came to William he became suddenly aware in his turn of William's scowling regard. He lifted his hat.

"Good afternoon," he said courteously.

"Afternoon," said William brusquely.

"Do you know," went on the man, "whether a—Miss Croft lives in the village?"

He pointed down the hill to the cluster of roofs.

"I think," said William slowly, "I've seen your photo—only you wasn't so old when you had it took."

"Where have you seen my photo?" said the man.

"In her house—wot I helped her to remove to," said William proudly.

The man's kind, rather weak face lit up.

"Could you show me her house? You see," he went on simply, "I'm a very unhappy man. I went away, but I've carried her in my heart all the time, but it's taken me a long, long time to find her. I'm a very tired, unhappy man."

William looked at him with some scorn.

"You was soft," he said. "P'raps it was 'cause of her hair not curlin'?"

"Where is she?" said the man.

"In there," said William, pointing to the enclosure sacred to the King of Fêtes. "I'll get her if you like."

"Thank you," said the man.

William, still grudging his entrance money, walked round the enclosure till he found a weak spot in the hedge behind a tent. Through this he scrambled with great difficulty, leaving his cap en route, blackening and scratching his face, tearing his knickers in two places, and his jersey in three. But William, who could not see himself, fingering tenderly the price of admission in his pocket, felt that it had been trouble well expended. He met the Vicar's wife. She was raffling a tea-cosy highly decorated with red and yellow and purple tulips on a green ground. She wore her Sale of Work smile. William accosted her.

"He wants her. He's come back. Could you get her?" he said. "He's had the right one in his inside all the time. He said so . . ."

But she had no use for William. William did not look as if he was good for a one-and-six raffle ticket for a tea-cosy.

"Sweet thing!" she murmured vaguely, and effusively

caressed his disordered hair as she passed.

William made his way towards the tent of the Woman of Mystery. But there was an ice-cream stall on his way and William could not pass it. Robert and Ethel, glasses of fashion and moulds of form, passed at the minute. At the sight of William with torn coat and jersey, dirty scratched face, no cap and tousled hair, consuming ice-cream horns among a crowd of his social inferiors, a shudder passed through both of them. They felt that William was a heavy handicap to them in Life's race.

"Send him home," said Robert.

"I simply wouldn't be seen speaking to him," replied Ethel.

William, having satisfied his craving for ice-cream with the greater part of his entrance money, wandered on towards the tent of the Woman of Mystery. He entered it by crawling under the canvas at the back. The Woman of Mystery happened to be having a slack time. The tent was empty.

"He's come," announced William. "He's waiting outside."

"Who?" said the Woman of Mystery.

"The one wot you've got a photo of. You know. He's jus' by the gate."

"Oh, dear!" gasped the Woman of Mystery. "Does he want me?"

"'Um," said William.

"Oh, dear!" fluttered the Woman of Mystery. "I must go—yet how can I go? People will be coming for their fortunes."

William waved aside the objection.

"Oh, I'll see to that," he said.

"But—can you tell fortunes, dear?" she asked.

"I dunno," said William. "I've never tried yet."

The Woman of Mystery drew off her curious gown.

AT THE SIGHT OF WILLIAM A SHUDDER PASSED THROUGH BOTH
OF THEM. THEY FELT THAT WILLIAM WAS A HEAVY HANDICAP
TO THEM IN LIFE'S RACE.

"I must go," she said.

With that she fled—through the back opening of the
tent.

William slowly and deliberately arrayed himself. He
put on the gown and arranged it so that his eyes came to
the two eye-holes and his hands out of the two armholes.
Then he lifted the hassock on which the Woman of
Mystery had disposed her feet, on to the chair, and took

his seat upon it, carefully hiding it with the gown. At that
moment the flap of the tent opened and a client entered.
She put half a crown on the table, and sat down on the
chair opposite William.

Peering through his eye-holes William recognised
Miss Drew.

He spread out a row of the playing-cards and began to
whisper. William's whisper was such a little known
quantity that it was not recognised.

"You've got a bad temper," he whispered.

"True!" sighed Miss Drew.

"You've got a cat and hens," went on William.

"True."

"You've been hard on a boy jus' lately. He—he may
not live very long. You've time to make up to him."

Miss Drew started.

"That's all."

Miss Drew, looking bewildered and troubled, withdrew from the tent.

William was surprised on peering through his
eyeholes to recognise Ethel in his next visitor. He spread
out the cards and began to whisper again.

"You've got two brothers," he whispered.

Ethel nodded.

"The small one won't live long prob'ly. You better be
kinder to him while he lives. Give in to him more. That's
all."

Ethel withdrew in an awed silence.

Robert entered next. William was beginning to enjoy
himself.

"You've gotter brother," he whispered. "Well, he's
not strong an' he may die soon. This is a warning for you.
You'd better make him happy while he's alive. That's
all."

"YOU'VE BEEN HARD ON A BOY JUS' LATELY. HE—HE MAY NOT
LIVE VERY LONG. YOU'VE TIME TO MAKE UP TO HIM."

Robert went slowly from the tent. At that moment the
little Woman of Mystery fluttered in from the back.

"Oh, thank you *so* much, dear. Such a *wonderful*
thing has happened. But I must return to my post. He'll
wait till the end, he says."

Still talking breathlessly, she drew the robe of mystery
from William and put it on herself.

William wandered out again into the Fête ground. He visited the ice-cream stall again, then wandered aimlessly around. The first person to accost him was Miss Drew.

"Hello, William," she said, gazing at him anxiously. "I've been looking for you. Would you like some ice-cream?"

William graciously condescended to be fed with ice-cream.

"Would you like a box of chocolates?" went on Miss Drew. "Do you feel all right, William, dear? You've been a bit pale lately."

William accepted from her a large box of chocolates and three donkey rides. He admitted that perhaps he hadn't been feeling very strong lately. When she departed he found Robert and Ethel looking for him. They treated him to a large and very satisfying tea and several more donkey rides. Both used an unusually tender tone of voice when addressing him. Ethel bought him a pine-apple and another box of chocolates, and Robert bought him a bottle of sweets and apologised for his unreasonable behaviour about the shoe polish. When they went home William walked between them and they carried his chocolates and sweets and pine-apple for him. Feeling that too much could not be made of the present state of affairs, he made Robert do his homework before he went to bed. Up in his room he gave his famous imitation of a churchyard cough that he had made perfect by practice and which had proved a great asset to him on many occasions. Ethel crept softly upstairs. She held a paper bag in her hand.

"William, darling," she said, "I've brought this toffee for your throat. It might do it good."

William added it to his store of presents.

"Thank you," he said with an air of patient suffering.

"And I'll give you something to make your wigwam

with to-morrow, dear," she went on.

"Thank you," said William.

"And if you want to practise your mouth-organ in the mornings it doesn't matter a bit."

"Thank you," said William in a small, martyred voice.

* * *

The next evening William walked happily down the road. It had been a very pleasant day. Miss Drew had done most of his work for him at school. He had been treated at lunch by his family with a consideration that was quite unusual. He had been entreated to have all that was left of the trifle while the rest of the family had stewed prunes.

In the garden of the little cottage was Miss Tabitha Croft and the tall, stooping man.

"Oh, this is William," said Miss Tabitha. "William is a *great* friend of mine!"

"I saw William yesterday," said the man. "William must certainly come to the wedding."

"William," said Miss Croft, "it was kind of you to take my place yesterday. Did you manage all right?"

"Yes," said William, after a moment's consideration, "I managed all right, thank you."

Chapter 4

William All the Time

William was walking down the road, his hands in his pockets, his mind wholly occupied with the Christmas pantomime. He was going to the Christmas pantomime next week. His thoughts dwelt on rapturous memories of previous Christmas pantomimes—of *Puss in Boots*, of *Dick Whittington*, of *Red Riding Hood*. His mouth curved into a blissful smile as he thought of the funny man—inimitable funny man with his red nose and enormous girth. How William had roared every time he appeared! With what joy he had listened to his uproarious songs! But it was not the funny man to whom William had given his heart. It was to the animals. It was to the cat in *Puss in Boots*, the robins in *The Babes in the Wood*, and the wolf in *Red Riding Hood*. He wanted to be an animal in a pantomime. He was quite willing to relinquish his beloved future career of pirate in favour of that of animal in a pantomime. He wondered . . .

It was at this point that Fate, who often had a special eye on William, performed one of her lightning tricks.

A man in shirt-sleeves stepped out of the wood and looked anxiously up and down the road. Then he took out his watch and muttered to himself. William stood still and stared at him with frank interest. Then the man began to stare at William, first as if he didn't see him, and then as if he saw him.

"Would you like to be a bear for a bit," he said.

William pinched himself. He seemed to be awake.

"A b-b-bear?" he queried, his eyes almost starting out of his head.

"Yes," said the man irritably, "a bear. B.E.A.R. bear, Animal—Zoo. Never heard of a bear?"

William pinched himself again. He seemed to be still awake.

"Yes," he agreed as though unwilling to commit himself entirely. "I've heard of a bear all right."

"Come on, then," said the man, looking once more at his watch, once more up the road, once more down the road, then turning on his heel and walking quickly into the wood.

William followed, both mouth and eyes wide open. The man did not speak as he walked down the path. Then suddenly down a bend in the path they came upon a strange sight. There was a hut in a little clearing, and round the hut was clustered a group of curious people—a Father Christmas, holding his beard in one hand and a glass of ale in the other; a rather fat Goldilocks, in the act of having yellow powder lavishly applied to her face, several fairies and elves, sucking large and redolent peppermints; a ferocious, but depressed-looking giant, rubbing his hands together and complaining of the cold; and several other strange and incongruous figures. In front of the hut was a large species of camera with a handle, and behind stood a man smoking a pipe.

"Kid turned up?" he said.

William's guide shook his head.

"No," he said, "they've missed their train or lost their way, or evaporated, or got kidnapped or something, but this happened to be passing, and it looked the same size pretty near. What do you think?"

The man took his pipe from his mouth in order the better to concentrate his whole attention on William. He looked at William from his muddy boots to his untidy head. Then he reversed the operation, and looked from his untidy head to his muddy boots. Then he scratched his head.

"Seems on the big side for the middle one," he said.

At this point a hullabaloo arose from behind the shed, and a small bear appeared, howling loudly.

"He tooken my bit of toffee," yelled the bear in a very human voice.

"Aw, shut up!" said the man in his shirt-sleeves.

SUDDENLY DOWN A BEND IN THE PATH THEY CAME UPON A
STRANGE SIGHT.

The small bear was followed by a large bear, protesting loudly.

"I gave him half'n mine 'n'e promised to give me half'n his' 'n' then he tried to eat it all'n'——"

"Aw, shut up!" repeated the man. Then he turned to William.

"All you gotter do," he said, "is to fix on the middle bear's suit an' do exactly what you're told, an' I'll give you five shillings at the end. See?"

"These roural places are a butiful chinge," murmured Goldilocks' mother, darkening her eyebrows as she spoke. "So calm and quart."

"These Christmas shows," grumbled the giant, flapping his arms vigorously, "are the very devil."

Here William found his voice. "Crumbs!" he ejaculated. Then, feeling the expletive to be altogether inadequate to the occasion, quickly added: "Gosh!"

"Take the kid round, someone," said the shirt-sleeve man wearily, "and fix on his togs, and let's get on with the show."

Here a Fairy Queen appeared from behind the hut.

"I don't see how I'm possibly to go through with this here performance," she said in a voice of plaintive suffering. "I had toothache all last night——"

"If you think," said the shirt-sleeve man, "that you can hold up this blessed show for a twopenny-halfpenny toothache——"

"If you're going to be insulting——" said the Fairy Queen in shrill indignation.

"Aw, shut up!" said the shirt-sleeve man.

Here Father Christmas, who had finished his ale, led William into the hut. A bear's suit lay on a chair.

"The kid wot was to wear this not having turned up," he said by way of explanation, "and you by all accounts bein' willin' to oblige for a small consideration, we shall have to see what can be done. I suppose," he added, "you have no objection?"

"Me?" said William, whose eyes and mouth had grown more and more circular every minute. "*Me*— objection? Golly! I should think *not*."

The little bear and the big bear surveyed him critically.

"He's too *big*," said the little bear contemptuously.

"His hair's too long," contributed the big bear.

"His face is too dirty."

"His ears is too long."

"His nose is too flat."

"His head's too big."

"His——"

William speedily and joyfully put an end to the duet and Father Christmas wearily disentangled the struggling mass.

"It may be a bit on the small side," he conceded as he deposited the small bear upside down beneath the table, "but we'll do what we can."

Here the shirt-sleeve man appeared at the window.

"That's right," he said kindly. "Take all day about it. Don't hurry! We all enjoy hanging about and waiting for you."

Father Christmas offered to retire from his post in favour of the shirt-sleeve man, and the shirt-sleeve man hastily retreated.

Then came the task of fitting William into the skin. It was not an easy task.

"You're bigger," said Father Christmas, "than what you look in the distance. Considerable."

William could not stand quite upright in the skin, but by stooping slightly he could see and speak through the open mouth of the head. In an ecstasy of joy he pummelled the big bear, the little bear gladly joined in the fray and a furry ball of three struggling bears rolled out of the door of the hut.

The shirt-sleeve man rang a bell.

"After this somewhat lengthy interlude," he said. "By the way, may I inquire the name of our new friend?"

William proudly shouted his name through the aperture in the bear's head.

"Well, Billiam," he said jocularly, "do just what I tell you and you'll be all right. Now all clear off a minute, please. We've only a few scenes to do here."

"Location," he read from a paper in his hand, "hut in wood. Enter fairies with Fairy Queen. Dance."

"How I am expected to dance," said the Fairy Queen bitterly, "tortured by toothache, I can't think."

"You don't dance with your teeth," said the shirt-sleeve man unsympathetically. "Let's go through it once before we turn on the machine. You've rehearsed it often enough. Now, come on."

They danced a dance that made William gape in surprise and admiration, so dainty and airy was it.

"Enter Father Christmas," went on the shirt-sleeve man.

"What I can't think," said Father Christmas, fastening on his beard, "is what a Father Christmas's doing in this effect."

"Nor a giant," said the giant sadly.

"It's for a Christmas show," said the shirt-sleeve man. "You've gotter have a Father Christmas in a Christmas show, or else how'd people know it's a Christmas show? And you've gotter have a giant in a fairy tale whether there is one in it or not."

Father Christmas joined the dance—gave presents to all the fairies, then retired behind the hut to his private store of refreshment.

"Enter Goldilocks," said the shirt-sleeve man. "Now, where the dickens is that kid?"

Goldilocks, fat, fairy and rosy, appeared from behind a tree where she had been eating bananas.

She peered down the middle bear's mouth.

"It's a new one," she said.

"The other hasn't turned up," said the man. "This is Billiam, who is taking on the middle one for the small consideration of five shillings."

"He's put out his tongue at me," she screamed in shrill indignation.

At this the big bear, whose adoration of Goldilocks was very obvious, closed with William, and Goldilocks' mother screamed shrilly.

The giant separated the two bears and Goldilocks came to the hut with an expression of patient suffering meant to represent intense physical weariness. She gave a start of joy at the sight of the hut, which apparently she did not see till she had almost passed it. She entered. She gave a second start of joy at the sight of three porridge plates. She tasted the first two and consumed the third. She wandered into the other room. She gave a third start of joy at the sight of three beds. She tried them all and went to sleep beautifully and realistically on the smallest. William was lost in admiration.

"Come on, bears," said the man in shirt-sleeves. "Billiam, walk between them. Don't jump. *Walk.* In at the door. That's right. Now, Billiam, look at your plate, then shake your head at the big bear."

Trembling with joy, William obeyed. The big bear, in the privacy of the open mouth, put out his tongue at William with a hostile grimace. William returned it.

"Now to the little one," said the man in shirt-sleeves. But William was still absorbed in the big one. Enraged by a particularly brilliant feat in the grimacing line which he felt he could not outshine, he put out a paw and tripped up the big bear's chair. The big bear promptly picked up a porridge plate and broke it on William's head. The little bear hurled himself ecstatically into the conflict. Father Christmas wearily returned to his work of separating them.

"If you aren't satisfied with your bonus," said the shirt-sleeve man to William, "take it out of me, not the scenery. You've just done about five shillings' worth of damage already. Now let's get on."

The rest of the scene went off fairly well, but William was growing bored. It wasn't half such fun as he thought it would be. He wasn't feeling quite sure of his five shillings after those smashed plates. The only thing for which he felt a deep and lasting affection, from which he felt he could never endure to be parted, was his bear-skin. It was rather small and very hot, but it gave him a thrill of pleasure unlike anything he had ever known before. He was a bear. He was an animal in a pantomime. He began to dislike immensely the shirt-sleeve man, and the hut, and the Fairy Queen, and the giant, and all the rest of them, but he loved his bear suit. It was while the giant was having a scene by himself that the brilliant idea came to William. He was standing behind a tree. No one was looking at him. He moved very quietly further away. Still no one looked at him. He moved yet further away and still no one looked at him. In a few seconds he was leaping and bounding through the wood alone in the world with the bear-skin. He was a bear. He was a bear in a wood. He ran. He jumped. He turned head over heels. He climbed a tree. He ran after a rabbit. He was riotously, blissfully happy. He met a boy who fled from him with echoing yells of terror, and to William it seemed as if he had drunk of ecstasy's very fount. He ran on and on, roaring occasionally, and

HE MET A BOY WHO FLED FROM HIM WITH YELLS OF TERROR,
AND TO WILLIAM IT SEEMED AS IF HE HAD DRUNK IN
ECSTASY'S VERY FOUNT.

occasionally rolling in the leaves. Then something
happened. He gave a particularly violent jump and
strained the skin which was already somewhat tight. The
skin did not burst, but the head came down very far on to
William's head and wedged itself tightly. He could not
see out of its open mouth now. He could just see out of
one of the eye-holes, but only just. His mouth was
wedged tightly in the head and he found he could not
speak plainly. He put up his paws and pulled at the head
to loosen it, but with no results. It was very tightly
wedged. William's spirits drooped. It was all very well
being a bear in a wood as long as one could change
oneself to a boy at will. It was a very different thing being
fastened to a bear-skin for life. He supposed that in
time, if he went on growing to a man, he'd burst the
bear-skin. On the other hand, he couldn't get to his
mouth now, so he couldn't eat, and he'd not be able to
grow at all. Starvation stared him in the face. He was

hungry already. He decided to return home and throw himself on the mercy of his family. Then he remembered that his family were all out that afternoon. His mother was at a mothers' meeting at the Vicarage. He decided to go straight to the Vicarage. Perhaps the united efforts of the mothers of the village might succeed in getting his head off. He went out from the woods on to the road but was discouraged by the behaviour of a woman who was passing. She gave an unearthly yell, tore a leg of mutton from her basket, flung it at William's head, and ran for dear life down the road, screaming as she went. William, much depressed, returned to the woods and reached the Vicarage by a circuitous route. Feeling too shy to ring the bell and interview a housemaid in his present costume, he walked round the house to the French windows of the dining-room where the meeting was taking place. He stood pathetically in the doorway of the window.

"Mother," he began plaintively in a muffled and almost inaudible voice, but it would have made little difference had he spoken in his usual strident tones. The united scream of the mothers' meeting would have drowned it. Never in the whole course of his life had William seen a room empty so quickly. It was like magic. Almost before his plaintive and muffled "Mother" had left his lips, the room was empty. Only two dozen overturned chairs, an overturned table, and several broken ornaments marked the line of retreat. The room was empty.

The entire mothers' meeting, headed by the vicar's wife and the vicarage cook and housemaid, were dashing down the main road of the village, screaming as they went. William sadly surveyed the desolate scene before him and retreated again to the woods. He leant against a tree and considered the whole situation.

NEVER IN THE WHOLE COURSE OF HIS LIFE HAD WILLIAM SEEN
A ROOM EMPTY SO QUICKLY.

"Hello, Billiam!"

Turning his head to a curious angle and peering out of one of the bear's eye-holes, he recognised Goldilocks.

"Hello!" he returned in a spiritless voice.

"Why did you run away?" she said.

"Dunno," he said. "I wanted the old skin. Wish I'd never seed it."

"You do talk funny," she said. "I can't hear what you say."

And so far was William's spirit broken that he only sighed.

"I saw you going," she went on, "and I went after you, but you ran so fast that I lost you. Then I went round a bit by myself. I say, they won't be able to get on with the old thing without us. I heard them shouting for us. Isn't it fun? An' I heard some people screaming in the road. What was that?"

William sighed again. Then he shouted: "Try'n pull my head loose. *Hard*."

She complied. She pulled till William yelled again.

"You've nearly took my ears off,' he said angrily in his muffled, sepulchral voice.

But the head was wedged on as tightly as ever.

She went to the edge of the wood and peered across the road.

"There's a place there," she said, "with lots of men in. Go'n' ask them."

William somewhat reluctantly (for his previous experiences had sadly disillusioned him with human nature in general) went through the trees to the roadside.

He looked back at the white-clad form of Goldilocks.

"Wait for me," he whispered hoarsely.

Anxious to attract as little notice as possible, he crept

on all fours round to the door of the public-house. He poked in his head nervously.

"Please, can some-'n——" he began politely, but in the clatter that arose the ghostly whisper was lost. Several glasses and a chair were flung at his head. Amid shoutings and uproar the innkeeper went for his gun, but on his return William had departed, and the innkeeper, who knew the better part of valour, contented himself with bolting the door and fetching sal-volatile for his wife. After a decent interval he unlocked the door and the inmates crept cautiously home one by one.

"A great, furious brute," they were heard to say. "Must have escaped from a circus——"

"If we hadn't been quick——"

"We ought to get up a party with guns——"

"Let's go and warn the school, or it'll get the kids——"

On reaching their homes most of them found their wives in hysterics on the kitchen floor after a hasty return from the mothers' meeting.

Meanwhile William sat beneath a tree in the wood in an attitude of utter despondency, his head on his paws.

"Why didn't you *tell* them," said Goldilocks impatiently.

"I tell everyone," said William. "Nobody'll *listen* to me. They make a noise and throw things. I'm go'n' home."

He rose and held out a paw. He felt utterly and miserably cut off from his fellow-men. He clung pathetically to Goldilocks' presence.

"Come with me," he said.

Hand in hand, a curious couple, they went through the woods to the back of William's house. "If I die," he said at once, "afore we get home, you'd better bury me. There's a spade in the back-garden."

He took her round to the shed in his back garden.

"You stay here," he whispered. "An' I'll try and get my head took off an' then get us somethin' to eat."

Cautiously and apprehensively he crept into the house. He could hear his mother talking to the cook in the kitchen.

"It stood right in the window," she was saying in a trembling voice. "Not a very big animal but so ferocious-looking. We got out just in time—it was just getting ready to spring. It——"

William crept to the open kitchen door and assumed his most plaintive expression, forgetting for the moment that his expression could not be seen. Just as he was opening his mouth to speak, cook turned round and saw him. The scream that cook emitted sent William scampering up to his room in utter terror.

"It's gone up—plungin' into Master William's room— the *brute!* Thank evving the little darlin's out playin'. Oh, mum, the cunnin' brute's a-shut the door. Oh, my! It turned me inside out—it did. Oh, I darsn't go an' lock it in, but that's what ought to be done——"

"We—we'll get someone with a gun," said Mrs. Brown weakly. "We—oh, here's the master."

Mr. Brown entered as she spoke. "I've got terrible news for you," he said.

Mrs. Brown burst into tears.

"Oh, John, nothing could be worse than—than— John, it's upstairs. Do get a gun—in William's room. And—oh, my goodness, suppose, he's there—suppose it's mangling him—*do* go——"

Mr. Brown sat calmly in his chair.

"William," he said, "has eloped with a *jeune première* and a bear-skin. An entire Christmas pantomime is searching the village for him. They've spent the afternoon searching the wood and now they are searching the village. Father Christmas is drinking ale in a pub. He discovered that William had paid it a visit. A Fairy Queen is sitting outside the pub complaining of toothache, and Goldilocks' mother is complimenting the vicar on the rural beauty of his village, in the intervals of weeping over the loss of her daughter. I gathered that William had visited the vicarage. There's a giant complaining of the cold, and a man in his shirt-sleeves whose language is turning the air blue for miles around. I was coming up from the station and was introduced to them as William's father. I had some difficulty in calming them, but I promised to do what I could to find the missing pair. I'm rather keen on finding William. I don't think I can do better than hand him over to them for a few minutes. As for the missing damsel——"

Mrs. Brown found her voice.

"Do you mean——?" she gasped feebly, "do you mean that it was William all the time?"

Mr. Brown rose wearily.

"Of course," he said. "Isn't everything *always* William all the time?"

Chapter 5

Aunt Jane's Treat

William was blest with many relations, though "blest" is not quite the word he would have used himself. They seemed to appear and disappear and reappear in spasmodic succession throughout the year. He never could keep count of them. Most of them he despised, some he actually disliked. The latter class reciprocated his feelings fervently. Great-Aunt Jane was one he had never seen, and so he suspended judgment on her. But he rather liked the sound of her name. He received the news that she was coming to stay over Christmas with indifference.

"All right," he said, "I don't care. She can come if she wants to."

She came.

She was tall and angular and precise. She received William's scowling greeting with a smile.

"Best wishes of the festive season, William," she murmured.

William looked at her scornfully.

"All right," he murmured.

However, his opinion of her rose the next morning.

"I'd like to give you some treat, William dear," she said at breakfast, "to mark the festive season—something quiet and orderly—as I don't approve of merry-making."

William looked at her kind, weak face, with the spectacles and scraped-back hair, and sighed. He thought that Aunt Jane would be enough to dispel the hilarity of any treat. Great-Aunt Jane's father had been a Plymouth Brother, and Great-Aunt Jane had been brought up to disbelieve in pleasure except as a potent aid of the devil.

William asked for a day in which to choose the treat. He discussed it with his friends.

"Well," advised Ginger, "you jolly well oughter choose something she can't muck up like when my aunt took me to a messy ole museum and showed me stones and things—no animals nor nuffin'."

"What about the Zoo?" said Henry.

The Zoo was suggested to Great-Aunt Jane, but she shuddered slightly. "I don't think I *could*," she said. "It's so *dangerous*, I always feel. Those bars look so fragile. I should never forgive myself if little William were mangled by wild beasts when in my care."

William sighed and called his friends together again.

"She won't go to the Zoo," said William. "Somethin' or other about bars an' mangles."

"Well, what about Maskelyne's and Devant's?" said Henry. "My uncle took me once. It's all magic."

William, much cheered at the prospect, suggested Maskelyne's that evening. Aunt Jane thought it over for some time, then shook her head.

"No, dear," she said. "I feel that these illusions aren't quite honest. They pretend to do something they really couldn't do, and it practically amounts to falsehood. They deceive the eye, and all deceit is wrong."

William groaned and returned to his advisory council.

"She's awful," he said gloomily. "She's cracky, I think."

They discussed the matter again. Douglas had seen a notice of a fair as he came along.

"Try that," he said. "There's merry-go-rounds an' shows an' cocoanut-shies an' all sorts. It oughter be all right."

That evening William suggested a fair. Aunt Jane looked frightened. "What exactly *happens* in a fair?" she said earnestly.

William had learnt tact.

"Oh," he said, "you just walk around and look at things."

"What *sort* of things do you look at?" said Aunt Jane.

"Oh, just stalls of gingerbreads an' lemonade."

It sounded harmless. Aunt Jane's face cleared.

"Very well," she said. "Of course, I could stand outside while you walked round. . . ."

But upon investigation it appeared that William's parents had not that perfect trust in William that William seemed to think was his due, and objected strongly to William's walking round by himself. So Aunt Jane steeled herself to dally openly with the evil power of Pleasure-making.

"We can be quite quick," she said, "and it doesn't sound very bad."

William reported progress to his council.

"It's all right," he said cheerfully. "The ole luny's going to the fair."

Then his cheerfulness departed.

"Though, when you come to think of it," he said, "it jolly well won't be much fun for *me*."

"Well," said Ginger, "s'pose we all try to go there the same time. We can leave your ole Aunt Jane somewhere an' go off, can't we?"

William brightened.

"That sounds better," he said. "I guess she'll be quite easy to leave."

                    *   *   *

Aunt Jane was so nervous that she did not sleep at all on the night before the day arranged for the treat. Never before in her blameless life had Aunt Jane deliberately entered a place of entertainment.

"I do hope," she murmured on the threshold, holding William firmly by the hand, "that there's nothing really *wrong* in it."

She was dressed in a long and voluminous black skirt, a long and voluminous black coat, and a small black hat, adorned with black ears of wheat, perched upon her prim little head.

Inside she stopped, bewildered. The glaring lights, the noise, the shouting, seemed to be drawing Aunt Jane's eyes out of her sockets and through her large, round spectacles.

"It isn't a bit what I thought, William," she said. "I imagined just stalls—just quiet, plain stalls. Why are they throwing balls about, William?"

"It's a cocoanut-shy," said William.

"Can—can anyone do it?" said Aunt Jane.

"Anyone can try," said William, "if they pay twopence."

"And what happens if they knock it off?"

"They get the cocoanut," explained William loftily.

"I—I wonder if it's very difficult," mused Aunt Jane.

At this moment a well-aimed ball sent a cocoanut rolling in the sawdust. Aunt Jane gave a little scream.

"Oh, he *did* it! He *did* it!" she cried. "I—I'd love to try. There—there can't be anything *wrong* in it."

With trembling fingers she handed the man twopence and took the three wooden balls. A sudden hush of

astonishment fell on the crowd when Aunt Jane's
curious figure came to the fore. At the first throw she
shook her hat crooked, at the second she shook a tail of
hair down, at the third she shook off her spectacles. The
third ball went wider of the mark than all the others, and
hit a young man on the shoulder. Seeing Aunt Jane,

AT THE FIRST THROW AUNT JANE SHOOK HER HAT CROOKED
. . . THE BYSTANDERS CHEERED HER LOUDLY.

however, he only smiled. She demanded another
twopenny-worth. The bystanders cheered her loudly.
The crowd round the cocoanut-shy stall grew. People
from afar thought it was an accident, and crowded up to
watch. Then they saw Aunt Jane and stayed.

At last, after her sixth shot, Aunt Jane, flushed and
panting and dishevelled, turned to William.

"It's much more difficult than it looks, William," she
said regretfully, as she straightened her hat and hair. "I
would have liked to have knocked one off."

"What about me?" said William coldly.

"Oh, yes," she said. "You must try, too." So she paid
another twopence, and William tried, too. But the
crowd began to melt away at once, and even the
proprietor began to look bored. William realised that he
was an anticlimax and felt dispirited.

"You should use more *force*, I think, William," said
Aunt Jane, "and more directness of aim."

William growled.

"Well, you didn't do it," he said aggressively.

"No," said Aunt Jane, "but I think with practice——"

Here William was cheered by the sight of Henry and
Douglas and Ginger, who had all managed to evade
lawful authority, and come to the help of William. They
had decided to hide from Aunt Jane and then abscond
with William. But Aunt Jane hardly saw them. She
hurried on ahead, her cheeks flushed, her eyes alight,
and her prim little hat awry.

"It has," she said, "a decidedly *inspiriting* effect, the
light and music and crowds—decidedly inspiriting."

She halted before a roundabout.

"I wonder if it's enjoyable," she said musingly. "The
circular motion, of course, might be monotonous."

However, she decided to try it. She paid for William

and Douglas, and Henry, and Ginger, and herself, and mounted a giant cock. It began. She clung on for dear life. It went faster and faster. There came a gleam into her eyes, a smile of rapture to her lips. Again the crowd gathered to watch her. She looked at the people as the roundabout slowed down.

"How happy they all look," she said innocently. "It's—it's quite a pleasant motion, isn't it? It seems a pity to get off."

She stayed on, clinging convulsively to the pole, with one elastic-sided boot waving wildly. She stayed on yet again. She seemed to find the circular motion anything but monotonous. It seemed to give her a joy that all her blameless life had so far failed to produce.

William and Ginger had to climb down, pale and rather unsteady. Henry and Douglas followed their example the next time it stopped. But still Aunt Jane

CLINGING CONVULSIVELY TO THE POLE WITH ONE
ELASTIC-SIDED BOOT WAVING WILDLY.

stayed on, smiling blissfully, her hat dangling over one ear. And still the crowd at the roundabout grew. The rest of the fair ground was comparatively empty. All the fun of the fair was centred on Aunt Jane.

At last she descended from her mount and joined the rather depressed-looking group of boys who were her escort.

"It's curious," she said, "how much pleasanter is a circular motion than a straight one. This is much more exhilarating than, say, a train journey. And, of course, the music adds to the pleasantness."

"Well," said William, "you jolly well stayed on."

"It seemed," she said, "such a pity to get off."

The little party moved from the roundabout followed by most of the crowd. The crowd liked Aunt Jane. They wouldn't have lost sight of her for anything. Aunt Jane, for the first time in her life, appealed to the British Public. William and his friends felt themselves to be in a curious position. They had meant to leave Aunt Jane to her fate and go off to their own devices. But it did not seem possible to leave Aunt Jane, because everything seemed to centre round Aunt Jane, and they would only have been at the back of the crowd instead of at the front. But they felt that their position as escort of Aunt Jane was not a dignified one. Moreover, their feats drew forth none of the applause which Aunt Jane's feats drew forth. They felt neglected by the world in general.

Aunt Jane was next attracted by the poster of the Fat Woman outside one of the tents. She fixed her spectacles sternly, and approached the man who was crying the charms of the damsel.

"Surely that picture is a gross exaggeration, my good man?" she said.

"Hexaggeration?" he repeated. "It isn't 'arf the truth. That's wot it isn't. It isn't 'arf the truth. We—we couldn't get 'er on the picture if we made 'er as big as wot she is. Hexaggeration? Why—she's a walkin' mountain, that's wot she is. A reg'lar walkin' mountain. Come in and see 'er. Come in and judge for yerselves. Jus' come in and see if wot I'm tellin' yer isn't gospel."

Somehow or other they were swept in. Aunt Jane sat on the front seat. She gazed intently upon the Fat Woman, who sat at her ease upon a small platform.

"She seems," said Aunt Jane, "unnaturally large, certainly."

The showman discoursed upon the size of the Fat Woman, and then invited the audience to draw near.

"Touch 'er if yer want," he said. "Touch 'er and see she's reel. No decepshun."

Aunt Jane drew near with the rest and accosted the showman.

"Has she ever tried any of those fat-reducing foods?" she said.

The man looked at William.

"Is she batty?" he said simply.

"If you'll give me her address I'll talk to my doctor about her. I think something might be done to make her less abnormal."

At this the walking mountain rose threateningly from her gilded couch.

"'Ere," she said, "'oo yer a-callin' nimes of? You tell me that. 'Oo yer a-giving of yer sauce to? You talk ter me strite art if yer wants to an' I'll talk ter yer back—not 'arf. Don't go a 'urlin' of yer hinsults at me through '*im*. My young man—'e'll talk ter yer, nah, if yer wants."

"'Er young man, he's the Strong Man in the next tent," explained the man. "They're fiancies, they are. An' 'e's the divil an' all to tackle, 'e is. I'd advise yer, as friend to friend, to clear, afore she calls of 'im.'"

But Aunt Jane, the imitation wheat in her hat trembling with emotion was already "clearing."

"They quite misunderstood," she said, as soon as she had "cleared." "The word 'abnormal' conveys no insult, surely. I think I'll return and explain. I'll refer them to the dictionary and the derivation of the word. It simply means something outside the usual rule. If——"

She was returning eagerly to the tent to explain, but found the entrance blocked by a crowd, so she was persuaded to postpone her explanation. Moreover, she had caught sight of the Hoop-la, and was anxious to have the system explained to her. William wearily explained it.

"Oh, I see," said Aunt Jane, "a test of dexterity and accuracy of aim. Shall we—shall we try?"

They tried. They tried till William was tired. She had determined to "get something" or die. The crowd was gathering again. They applauded her efforts. Aunt Jane was too short-sighted to notice the crowd, but she heard its shouts.

"Isn't everyone *encouraging?*" she murmured to William. "It's most gratifying. It's really a very pleasant place."

She actually did get something. One of her wildly-flung hoops fell over a tie-pin of the extremely flashy variety, which she received with glowing pride and handed to William. The crowd cheered, but Aunt Jane was quite oblivious of the crowd.

"Come along," she said. "Let's do something else."

Ginger disconsolately announced his intention of going home. Henry and Douglas followed his example, and William was left alone to escort Aunt Jane through the mazes of the Land of Pleasure. It was at this point that things really seemed to go to Aunt Jane's head. She went down the Helter Skelter four or five times—sailing

WILLIAM WAS LEFT ALONE TO ESCORT AUNT JANE THROUGH
THE MAZES OF THE LAND OF PLEASURE.

down on her little mat with squeaks of joy. She forgot now to straighten her hat or her hair. Her eye gleamed with a strange light, her cheeks were flushed.

"There's something quite rejuvenating about it all, William," she murmured. She had her fortune told by a Gipsy Queen, who prophesied an early marriage with one of her many suitors.

She went again on the Roundabout, she had another cocoanut-shy, she went on the Switchback, the Fairy Boat, and the Wild Sea Waves. William trailed along behind her. He refused to venture on the Wild Sea Waves, and watched her on them with a certain grudging admiration.

"Crumbs!" he murmured, "she must have gotter inside of *iron!*"

Finally Aunt Jane espied a stall at a distance. Under a flaring gas-flame a man in a white coat was pulling out long strings of soft candy. Aunt Jane approached.

"What an appetising odour!" commented Aunt Jane. "Do you think he's *selling* it?" William thought he was.

And the glorious climax of that strange night was the sight of Aunt Jane standing under the flaring gas-jet devouring soft pull-out candy.

"'Ullo! 'Ere's the gime old bird," said a man passing.

"I don't see any bird, do you?" said Aunt Jane to William, peering round with her short-sighted eyes, "but this is a very palatable confection, is it not?"

Then a clock struck, and into Aunt Jane's face came the look that Cinderella's face must have worn when the clock struck twelve.

"William," she said, "that surely was not ten?"

"*Sounded* like ten," said William.

Aunt Jane put down her last stick of pull-out candy unfinished.

"We—we ought to go," she said weakly.

*   *   *

"Well," said William's mother when they returned. "I do hope it wasn't too tiring for you."

Aunt Jane sat down on a chair and thought. She thought over the evening. No, she couldn't really have done all that—have seen all that. It was impossible— quite impossible. It must be imagination. She must have seen someone else doing all those things. She must have gone quietly round with William and watched him enjoy himself. Of course that was all she'd done. It must have been. The other was unthinkable.

So she smiled, a patient, weary little smile.

"Well, of course," she said, "I'm a little tired but I think William enjoyed it."

Chapter 6

"Kidnappers"

There was quite a flutter in the village when the d'Arceys came to the Grange. A branch of *the* d'Arcey family, you know. Lord d'Arcey and Lady d'Arcey and Lady Barbara d'Arcey. Lady Barbara was seven years of age. She was fair, frilly, fascinating. Lady d'Arcey engaged a dancing-master to come down from London once a week to teach her dancing. They invited several of the children of the village to join. They invited William. His mother was delighted, but William—freckled, untidy, and seldom clean—was horrified to the depth of his soul. No entreaties or threats could move him. He said he didn't care what they did to him; he said they could kill him if they liked. He said he'd rather be killed than go to an ole dancing class anyway, with that soft-looking kid. Well, he didn't care who her father was. She *was* a soft-looking kid, and he wasn't going to *no* dancing class with her. Wildly ignoring the rules that govern the uses of the negative, he frequently reiterated that he *wasn't* going to *no* dancing class with her. He wouldn't be seen speaking to her, much less dancing with her.

His mother almost wept.

"You see," she explained to Ethel, William's grown-up sister, "it puts us at a sort of disadvantage. And Lady d'Arcey is so *nice*, and it's *so kind* of them to ask William!"

William's sister, however, took a wholly different view of the matter.

"It might put them," she said, "a good deal more against us if William *went!*"

William's mother admitted that there was something in that.

* * *

William lay in the loft, reclining at length on his front, his chin resting on his hands. He was engaged in reading. On one side of him stood a bottle of liquorice water, which he had made himself; on the other was a large slab of cake, which he had stolen from the larder. On his freckled face was the look of scowling ferocity that it always wore in any mental effort. The fact that his jaws had ceased to work, though the cake was yet unfinished, testified to the enthralling interest of the story he was reading.

"Black-hearted Dick dragged the fair maid by the wrist to the captain's cave. A bottle of grog stood at the

WILLIAM LAY IN THE LOFT—HIS CHIN RESTING ON HIS HANDS, READING.

captain's right hand. The captain slipped a mask over his eyes, and smiled a sinister smile. He twirled his long black moustachios with one hand.

"'Unhand the maiden, dog,' he said.

"Then he swept her a stately bow.

"'Fair maid,' he said, 'unless thy father bring me sixty thousand crowns to-night, thy doom is sealed. Thou shalt swing from yon lone pine-tree!'

"The maiden gave a piercing scream. Then she looked closely at the masked face.

"'Who—who art thou?' she faltered.

"Again the captain's sinister smile flickered beneath the mask.

"'Rudolph of the Red Hand,' he said.

"At these terrible words the maiden swooned into the arms of Black-hearted Dick.

"'A-ha,' said the grim Rudolph, with a sneer. 'No man lives who does not tremble at those words.'

"And again that smile curved his dread lips, as he looked at the yet unconscious maiden.

"For well he knew that the sixty thousand crowns would be his that even.

"'Let her be treated with all courtesy—till to-night,' he said as he turned away."

William heaved a deep sigh and took a long draught of liquorice water.

It seemed an easy and wholly delightful way of earning money.

*　　*　　*

"They're awfully nice people," said Ethel the next day at breakfast, "and it is so kind of them to ask us to tea."

"Very," said Mrs. Brown, "and they say, 'Bring the little boy'."

The little boy looked up, with the sinister smile he had been practising.

"Me?" he said. "Ha!"

He wished he had a mask, because, though he felt he could manage the smile quite well, the narrative had said nothing about the expression of the upper part of Rudolph of the Red Hand's face. However, he felt that his customary scowl would do quite well.

"You'll come, dear, won't you?" said Mrs. Brown sweetly.

"I wouldn't make him," said Ethel nervously. "You know what he's like sometimes."

Mrs. Brown knew. William—a mute, scowling protest—was no ornament to a drawing-room.

"But wouldn't you like to meet the little girl?" said Mrs. Brown persuasively.

"Huh!" ejaculated William.

The monosyllable looks weak and meaningless in print. As William pronounced it, it was pregnant with scorn and derision and sinister meaning. He curled imaginary moustachios as he uttered it. He looked round upon his assembled family. Then he uttered the monosyllable again with a yet more sinister smile and scowl. He wondered if Rudolph of the Red Hand had a mother who tried to make him go out to tea. He decided that he probably hadn't. Life would be much simpler if you hadn't.

With another short, sharp "Ha!" he left the room.

*   *   *

William sat on an old packing-case in a disused barn.

Before him stood Ginger, who shared the same class-room in school and pursued much the same occupations and recreations out of school. They were not a popular couple in the neighbourhood.

William was wearing a mask. The story had not stated what sort of mask Rudolph of the Red Hand had worn, but William supposed it was an ordinary sort of mask. He had one that he'd bought last Fifth of November, and it seemed a pity to waste it. Moreover, it had the advantage of having moustachios attached. It covered his nose and cheeks, leaving holes for his eyes. It represented fat, red, smiling cheeks, an enormous red nose, and fluffy grey whiskers. William, on looking at himself in the glass, had felt a slight misgiving. It had been appropriate to the festive season of November 5th, but he wondered whether it was sufficiently sinister to represent Rudolph of the Red Hand. However, it was a mask, and he could turn his lips into a sinister smile under it, and that was the main thing. He had definitely and finally embraced a career of crime. On the table before him stood a bottle of liquorice water with an irregularly printed label: GROG. He looked round at his brave.

"Black-hearted Dick," he said, "you gotter say, 'Present'."

He was rather vague as to how outlaws opened their meetings, but this seemed the obvious way.

"Present," said Ginger, "an' it's not much fun if it's all goin' to be like school."

"Well, it's *not*," said William firmly, "an' you can have a drink of grog—only one swallow," he added anxiously, as he saw Black-hearted Dick throwing his head well back preparatory to the draught.

"That was a jolly big one," he said, torn between admiration at the feat and annoyance at the disappearance of his liquorice water.

"All right," said Ginger modestly. "I've gotter big throat. Well, what we goin' to do first?"

William adjusted his mask, which was not a very good

"BLACK-HEARTED DICK," HE SAID, "YOU'VE GOTTER SAY
'PRESENT'."

fit, and performed the sinister smile.

"We gotter kidnap someone first," he said.

"Well, who?" said Ginger.

"Someone who can pay us money for 'em."

"Well, who?" said Ginger irritably.

William took a deep draught of liquorice water.

"Well, you can think of someone."

"I like that," said Ginger, in tones of deep dissatisfaction. "I *like* that. You set up to be captain and wear that thing, and drink up all the liquorice water——"

"Grog," William corrected him, wearily.

"Well, grog, an' then you don't know who we've gotter kidnap. I like that. Might as well be rat hunting or catching tadpoles or chasin' cats, if you don't know what we've gotter do."

William snorted and smiled sneeringly beneath his bilious-looking mask.

"Huh!" he said. "You come with me and I'll find someone for you to kidnap right enough."

Ginger cheered up at this news, and William took another draught of liquorice water. Then he hung up his mask behind the barn door and took out of his pocket a battered penknife.

"We may want arms," he said; "keep your dagger handy."

He pulled his school cap low down over his eyes. Ginger did the same, then looked at the one broken blade of his penknife.

"I don't think mine would *kill* anyone," he said. "Does it matter?"

"You'll have to knock yours on the head with something," said Rudolph of the Red Hand grimly. "You know we may be imprisoned, or hung, or somethin', for this."

"Rather!" said Ginger, with the true spirit of the

bravado, "an' I don't care."

They tramped across the fields in silence, William leading. In spite of his occasional exasperation, Ginger had infinite trust in William's capacity for attracting adventure.

They walked down the road and across a stile. The stile led to a field that bordered the Grange. Suddenly they stopped. A small white figure was crawling through a gap in the hedge from the park into the field. William had come out with no definite aim, but he began to think that Fortune had placed in his way a tempting prize. He turned round to his follower with a resonant "'Sh!", scowled at him, placed his finger on his lips, twirled imaginary moustachios, and pulled his cap low over his eyes. Through the trees inside the park he could just see the figure of a nurse on a seat leaning against a tree trunk in an attitude of repose. Suddenly Lady Barbara looked up and espied William's fiercely scowling face.

She put out her tongue.

William's scowl deepened.

She glanced towards her nurse on the other side of the hedge. Her nurse still slumbered. Then she accosted William.

"Hello, funny boy!" she whispered. Rudolph of the Red Hand froze her with a glance.

"Quick!" he said. "Seize the maiden and run!"

With a dramatic gesture he seized the maiden by one hand, and Ginger seized the other. The maiden was not hard to seize. She ran along with little squeals of joy.

"Oh, what fun! What fun!" she said.

Inside the barn, William closed the door and sat at his packing-case. He took a deep draught of liquorice water and then put on his mask. His victim gave a wild scream of delight and clapped her hands.

"Oh, *funny* boy!" she said.

William was annoyed.

"It's not funny," he said irritably. "It's jolly well not funny. You're kidnapped. That's what you are. Unhand the maiden, dog," he said to Ginger.

Ginger was looking rather sulky. "All right, I'm not handing her," he said, "an' when you've quite finished with the liquorice water——"

"Grog," corrected William, sternly.

"Well, grog, then, an' I helped to make it, p'raps you'll let me have a drink."

William handed him the bottle, with a flourish.

"Finish it, dog," he said, with a short, scornful laugh.

The vibration of the short, scornful laugh caused his bacchic mask (never very secure) to fall off on to the packing-case. Lady Barbara gave another scream of ecstasy.

"Oh, do it *again*, boy," she said.

William glanced at her coldly, and put on the mask again. Then he swept her a stately bow, holding on to his mask with one hand.

"Fair maiden," he said, "unless thy father bring me sixty thousand crowns by to-night, thy doom is sealed. Thou shalt swing from yon lone pine."

He pointed dramatically out of the window to a diminutive hawthorn hedge.

The captive whirled round on one foot, fair curls flying.

"Oh, he's going to make me a swing! *Nice* boy!"

William rose, majestic and stately, still cautiously holding his mask. "My name," he said, "is Rudolph of the Red Hand."

"Well, I'll *kiss* you, dear Rudolph Hand," she said, "if you like."

William's look intimated that he did not like.

"Oh, you're *shy!*" said Lady Barbara, delightedly.

"FAIR MAID," HE SAID, "UNLESS THY FATHER BRING ME SIXTY
THOUSAND CROWNS, THOU SHALT SWING FROM YON LONE
PINE."

"Let her be treated," William said, "with all courtesy till this even."

"Well," said Ginger, "*that's* all right, but what we goin' to do with her?"

William glanced disapprovingly at the maiden, who had turned the packing-case upside down and was sitting in it.

"Well, what we goin' to do?" said Ginger. "It's not much fun so far."

"Well, we just gotter wait till her people send the money."

"Well, how they goin' to know we got her, and where she is, an' how much we want?"

William considered. This aspect of the matter had not struck him.

"Well," he said at last. "I s'pose you'd better go an' tell them."

"You can," said Ginger.

"You'd better go," said William, "'cause I'm chief."

"Well, if you're chief," said Ginger, "you oughter go."

The kidnapped one emitted a shrill scream.

"I'm a train," she said. "Sh! Sh! Sh!"

"She's not actin' right," said William severely; "she oughter be faintin' or somethin'."

"How much do we want for her?"

"Sixty thousand crowns," said William.

"All right," said Ginger. "I'll stay and see she don't get away, an' you go an' tell her people, an' don't tell anyone but her father and mother, or they'll go gettin' the money themselves."

William hung up his mask behind the door and turned to Ginger, assuming the scowl and attitude of Rudolph of the Red Hand.

"All right," he said, "I'll go into the jaws of death,

and you treat her with all courtesy till even."

"Who's goin' to curtsey?" said Ginger indignantly.

"You don't understand book talk," said William scornfully.

He bowed low to the maiden, who was still playing at trains.

"Rudolph of the Red Hand," he said slowly, with a sinister smile.

The effect was disappointing. She blew him a kiss.

"Darlin' Rudolph," she said.

William stalked majestically across the fields towards the Grange, with one hand inside his coat, in the attitude of Napoleon on the deck of the *Bellerophon*.

He went slowly up the drive and up the broad stone steps. Then he rang the bell. He rang it with the mighty force with which Rudolph of the Red Hand would have rung it. It pealed frantically in distant regions. An indignant footman opened the door.

"I wish to speak to the master of the house on a life or death matter," said William importantly.

He had thought out that phrase on the way up.

The footman looked him up and down. He looked him up and down as if he didn't like him.

"Ho! *do* you!" he said. "And hare you aware as you've nearly broke our front-door bell?"

The echoes of the bell were just beginning to die away.

Rudolph of the Red Hand folded his arms and emitted a short, sharp laugh.

"His Lordship," said the footman, preparing to close the door, "is *hout*."

"His wife would do, then," said Rudolph. "Jus' tell her it's a life an' death matter."

"Her Ladyship," said the footman, "is hengaged, and hany more of your practical jokes 'ere, my lad, and you'll hear of it." He shut the door in William's face.

William wandered round the house and looked in several of the windows; he had a lively encounter with a gardener, and finally, on peeping into the kitchen regions with a scornful laugh, was chased off the premises by the unfuriated footman. Saddened, but not defeated, he returned across the fields to the barn and flung open the door. Ginger, panting and perspiring, was dragging the Lady Barbara in the packing-case round and round the barn by a piece of rope.

He turned a frowning face to William. A life of crime was proving less exciting than he had expected.

"Well, where's the money?" he said, wiping his brow. "She's jus' about wore me out. She won't let me stop draggin' this thing about. An' she keeps worrin', sayin' you promised her a swing."

"He *did!*" said the kidnapped one shrilly.

"Well, where's the money?" repeated Ginger. "I've jus' about had enough of kidnappin'."

"I couldn't *get* the money," said William. "I couldn't make 'em listen properly. Let's change, an' me stay here an' you go and get the money."

"All right," said Ginger. "I wun't mind changing to do anything from this. What shall I say to 'em?"

"You'd better say you must speak to 'em on life or death. I said that, but they kind of didn't listen. They'll p'raps listen to you."

"Well, I jolly well don't mind goin'," said Ginger; "she's a *wearin*' kid."

He went out and shut the door.

"Put the funny thing on your face," ordered Lady Barbara.

"It's not funny," said William coldly, as he adjusted the mask.

She danced round him, clapping her hands.

"Dear, *funny* boy! An' now make me the swing."

"I'm not goin' to make you no swing," said William firmly.

"If you don't make me a swing," she said, "I'll sit down an' I'll scream an' scream till I burst."

She began to grow red in the face.

"There's no rope," said William hastily.

She pointed to a coil of old rope in a dark corner of the barn.

"That's rope, silly," she said.

He took it out and began to look round for a suitable and low enough tree.

"Be *quick!*" ordered his victim.

At last he had the rope tied up.

"Now lift me in! Now swing me! Go on! *More! More* More! Nice, funny boy!"

She kept him at that for about half an hour. Then she demanded to be dragged round the barn in the packing-case.

"Go *on!*" she said. "*Quicker! Quicker!*"

The fine, manly spirit of Rudolph of the Red Hand was almost broken. He began to look weary and disconsolate.

When Ginger returned, Lady Barbara was wearing the mask and chasing William.

"Go on!" she said, "'tend to be frightened. 'Tend to be frightened. Go on!"

William turned to Ginger.

"Well?" he said.

Ginger looked rather dishevelled. His collar was torn away.

"You might have told me," he said indignantly.

"What?" said William.

"Go *on!*" said Lady Barbara.

"That they were like wild beasts up there. They set on

me soon as I said what you told me."

"Well, did you get any money?" said William.

"Now, how could I?" said Ginger irritably, "when they set on me like wild beasts soon as I said it."

"Go *on!*" said Lady Barbara.

"Well," said Rudolph of the Red Hand, slowly. "I'm jus' about fed up."

"An' you cudn't be fed upper than I am," replied his gallant brave.

"Well, let's chuck it," said William. "It's getting tea-time, an' we've got no money, an' I'm not going for it again."

"Nor'm I," said Ginger fervently.

"An' I'm fed up with this kid."

"So'm I," said Ginger still more fervently.

"Well, let's chuck it."

He turned to Lady Barbara. "You can go home," he said.

Her face fell.

"I don't *want* to go home," she said; "I'm going to stay with you always and always."

"Well, you're not," said William shortly, "'cause we're going home—so there."

He set off with Ginger across the fields. The kidnapped one ran lightly beside them.

"I'm going where you go," she said. "I *like* you."

They felt that her presence would be difficult to explain to their parents. Dejectedly, they returned to the barn.

"I'll go an' see if I can see anyone looking for her," said William.

"Get down on your hands and knees and let me ride on your back," shouted Lady Barbara. Ginger wearily obeyed.

William went out to the road and looked up it and

down. There was no one there, except a man walking in the direction of the Grange. He smiled at the expression on William's face.

"Hello!" he said, "feeling sick, or lost something?"

"We kidnapped a kid," said William disconsolately, "an' we cudn't get any money for her, an' we can't get rid of her."

The man threw back his head and laughed.

"Awkward!" he said, "by Jove—jolly awkward! I suppose you'll have to take her home."

He was no use.

William turned back to the barn. Lady Barbara was riding round the barn on Ginger's back.

"Go *on!*" she said. "*Quicker!*"

"WE KIDNAPPED A KID," SAID WILLIAM DISCONSOLATELY,
"AN' WE CUDN'T GET ANY MONEY FOR HER, AN' WE CAN'T GET
RID OF HER."

Ginger turned a purple and desperate face to William. "If you don't do something soon," he said, "I shall probably go mad and kill someone."

"We'll have to take her back," said William grimly.

The kidnappers walked in gloomy silence; the kidnapped danced along between them, holding a hand of each.

"I'm going wherever you go," she said; "I love you."

Once Ginger spoke.

"*You're* a nice kidnapper," he said bitterly.

"I cudn't help it," said William. "It all went different in the book."

Near the steps of the front door a lady was standing.

Ginger turned and fled at the sight of her. Lady Barbara held William's hand fast. William hesitated till flight was impossible.

"Oh, *there* you are, darling," the lady said.

"Dear, nice boy," said Lady Barbara. "He's been playing with me all the time. And the other—but the other's gone. It's been lovely. I *do* love him. May we keep him?"

"Darling," said the lady, "I've only just heard you were lost. Nanny's in a dreadful state. And this little boy found you and took care of you? *Dear* little boy!"

She bent down and kissed the outraged and horrified William. "How *very* kind of you to look after my little girl and bring her back so nicely. Now come and have some tea."

She led William, too broken in spirit to resist, up the steps into the hall, then into a room. Lady Barbara still held his hand tightly. There was tea in the room and *people*. Horror of horrors! It was his mother and Ethel. There were confused explanations.

"And her nurse went to sleep, and she must have wandered off and got lost, and your little boy found her, and played with her, and looked after her, and brought her back for tea. *Dear* little man!"

A man entered—the man who had accosted William on the road. He was evidently the father of the little girl. The story was repeated to him.

"Great!" he said, looking at William with amusement and a certain sympathy in his eye. He seemed to be enjoying the situation. William glared at him.

"An' he rode me on his back, and gave me rides in the box, and made me a swing, and put on a funny face to make me laugh."

"*Dear* little man!" crooned Lady d'Arcey.

They put him gently into a chesterfield, and Barbara sat beside him, leaning against him.

"Nice boy," she said.

Mrs. Brown and Ethel beamed proudly.

"And he *pretends*," said Mrs. Brown, "not to like little girls. We misjudge children so sometimes. You'll go to the dancing class *now*, won't you, dear?" she ended archly.

"*Dear* little fellow!" said Lady d'Arcey.

It was only the fact that he had no weapon in his hand that he had given up the unequal struggle against the malignancy of Fate that saved William from murder on a wholesale scale.

Barbara smiled on him fondly. Barbara's mother smiled on him tenderly, his mother and sister smiled on him proudly, and in their midst Rudolph of the Red Hand, with rage and shame and humiliation in his heart, savagely ate his sugared cake.

Chapter 7

William's Evening Out

William's family had come up to London for a holiday. They had brought William with them chiefly because it was not safe to leave William behind. William was not the sort of boy who could be trusted to live a quiet and blameless life at home in the absence of his parents. He had many noble qualities, but he had not that one. So William gloomily and reluctantly accompanied his family to London.

William's elder sister and mother lived in a whirl of shopping and theatres; William's elder brother went every day to see a county cricket match, and returned in a state of frenzied excitement to discuss the play and players all the evening without the slightest encouragement from any one; William's father foregathered with old cronies at his club or slept in the hotel smoking-room.

It was open to William to accompany any of the members of his family. He might shop and attend *matinées* with his mother and Ethel, he might go (on sufferance) to watch cricket matches with Robert, or he might sleep in the smoking-room with his father.

He was encouraged by each of them to join some other member of the family, and he occasionally managed to evade them all and spend the afternoon sliding down the banisters (till firmly, but politely, checked by the manager of the hotel), watching for any temporary absence of the liftman during which he might try to manipulate the machine itself or contending with the most impudent-looking page-boy in a silent and furtive rivalry in grimaces. But, in spite of this, he was supremely bored. He regarded the centre of the British Empire with contempt.

"*Streets!*" he said, with devastating scorn, at the end of his first day here. "*Shops!* Huh!"

William's soul pined for the fields and lanes and wood of his home; for his band of boon companions, with whom he was wont to wrestle, and fight, and trespass, and plot dare-devil schemes, and set the world at defiance; for the irate farmers who helped to supply that spice of danger and excitement without which life to William and his friends was unendurable.

He took his London pleasures sadly.

"Oh—*history!*" he remarked coldly, when they escorted him round Westminster Abbey. His only comment on being shown the Tower was that it seemed to be takin' up the whole day, not that there was much else to do, anyway.

His soul yearned for the society of his own kind. The son of his mother's cousin, who lived near, had come to see him one day. He was a tall, pale boy, who asked William if he could fox-trot, and if he didn't adore Axel Haig's etchings, and if he didn't prefer Paris to London. The conversation was an unsatisfactory one, and the acquaintance did not ripen.

But, accompanying his family on various short cuts in the back streets of London, he had glimpsed another world, a world of street urchins, who fought and wrestled, and gave vent to piercing whistles, and hung on to the backs of carts, and paddled in the gutter, and rang front-door bells and fled from policemen. He

watched it wistfully. Socially, his tastes were not high.
All he demanded from life was danger and excitement
and movement and the society of his own kind. He liked
boys, crowds of boys, boys who shouted and whistled
and ran and courted danger, boys who had never heard
of any silly old etchings.

As he followed his family with his air of patient
martyrdom on all their expeditions, it was the glimpse of
this underworld alone that would lift the shadow from
his furrowed brow and bring a light to his stern, freckled
countenance . . . There were times when he stopped
and tried to get into contact with it, but it was not
successful. His mother's "Come along, William. Don't
speak to those horrid little boys," always recalled him to
the blameless and palling respectability of his own
family. Yet even before that hateful cry interrupted him
he knew that it was useless.

He was an alien being—a clean little boy in a neat suit,
with a fashionable mother and sister. He was beyond the
pale, an outsider, a pariah, a creature to be mocked and
jeered at. The position galled William. He was, by
instinct, on the side of the lawless—the anti-respectable.

His spirits rose as the time for his return to the country
approached. Yet there was a wistful longing at his heart
for the boy world at London still unexplored, as well as a
fierce contempt for the London his parents had revealed
to him.

*   *   *

William had been invited to a party on his last evening
in London. William's mother's cousin lived in Kensing-
ton, and had invited William to a "little gathering of her
children's friends". William did not wish to go to the
party. What is more, William did not intend to go to the

party. But a wonderful plan had come into William's head.

"It's very kind of her," he said meekly. "Yes, I'll be very pleased to go."

This was unlike William's usual manner of receiving an invitation to a party. Generally there were expostulations, indignation, assertion of complete incapacity to go to anything that particular night. William's mother looked at him.

"You—you feel all right, don't you, dear?" she said anxiously.

"Oh, yes," said William, "an' I feel I'd jus' like a party."

"You can wear your Eton suit," said Mrs. Brown.

"Oh, yes," said William. "I'd like that."

William's face was quite expressionless as he spoke. Mrs. Brown pinched herself to make sure that she was awake.

"I expect they'll have music and dancing and that sort of thing," she said.

She thought, perhaps, that William had misunderstood the kind of party it would be.

William's expressionless face did not change.

"Oh, yes," he said pleasantly, "music and dancin' will be fine."

When Mr. Brown was told of the invitation he groaned.

"And I suppose it will take the whole day to make him go," he said.

"No," said Mrs. Brown eagerly. "That's the strange part. He seems to *want* to go. He really does. And he seems to *want* to wear his Eton suit, and you know what a bother that used to be. I suppose he's beginning to take a pride in his appearance. I think London must be civilising him."

"Well," said Mr. Brown, dryly, "I suppose you know best. I suppose miracles do happen."

When the evening of the party arrived, there was some difficulty as to the transit of William to his place of entertainment. The house was so near to the hotel where the Browns were staying that a taxi seemed hardly worth while. But there was a general reluctance to be his escort.

Ethel was going to a theatre, and Robert had been out all day and thought he deserved a bit of rest in the evening, instead of carting kids about, Mrs. Brown's rheumatism had come on again, and Mr. Brown wanted to read the evening paper.

William, sleek and smooth, and brushed and encased in his Eton suit, his freckled face shining with cleanliness and virtue, broke meekly into the discussion.

"I know the way, mother. Can't I just go myself?"

Mrs. Brown wavered.

"I don't see why not," she said at last.

"If you think that boy can walk three yards by himself without getting into mischief——" began Mr. Brown.

William turned innocent, reproachful eyes upon him.

"Oh, but *look* at him," said Mrs. Brown; "and it isn't as if he didn't want to go to the party. You want to go, don't you, dear?"

"Yes, mother," said William, meekly.

His father threw him a keen glance.

"Well, of course," he said, returning to his paper, "do as you like. I'm certainly not going with him myself, but don't blame me if he blows up the Houses of Parliament or dams the Thames, or pulls down Nelson's Monument."

William's sorrowful, wistful glance was turned again upon his father.

"I won't do any of those things, I promise, father," he

said solemnly.

"I don't see why he shouldn't go alone," said Mrs. Brown. "It's not far, and he's sure to be good, because he's looking forward to it so; aren't you, William?"

"Yes, mother," said William, with his most inscrutable expression.

So he went alone.

*   *   *

William set off briskly down the street—a neat figure in an Eton suit, an overcoat, a well-fitting cap and patent leather shoes.

His expression had relaxed as soon as the scrutiny of his family was withdrawn. It became expectant and determined.

Once out of the sight of possible watchers from the hotel, he turned off the road that led to his mother's cousin's house, and walked purposefully down a side street and thence to another side street.

There they were. He knew they would be there. Boys—boys after William's own heart—dirty boys, shouting boys, whistling boys, fighting boys. William approached. At his own home he would have been acclaimed at once as leader of any lawless horde. But here he was not known. His present appearance, moreover—brushed hair, evening clothes, clean face— was against him. To them he was a thing taboo. They turned on him with delightful yells of scorn.

"Yah!"

"Where's yer mammy?"

"Look at 'is shoes! Boo-oo!"

"*Isn't* 'is 'air brushed nice?"

"Yah!"

"Boo!"

"Garn!"

The tallest of them snatched William's cap from his head and ran off with it. The snatching of a boy's cap from his head is a deadly insult. William, whose one wistful desire was to be friends with his new acquaintances, yet had his dignity to maintain. He flew after the boy and caught him by the back of his neck. Then they closed.

The rest of the tribe stood round them in a ring, giving advice and encouragement. The contempt for William vanished. For William was a good fighter. He lost his collar and acquired a black eye; and his hair, in the exhilaration of the contest, recovered from its recent severe brushing and returned to its favourite vertical angle.

The two were fairly well matched, and the fight was a most satisfactory one till the cry of "Cops" brought it to an abrupt end, and the crowd of boys, with William now in the middle, fled precipitately down another street. When they were at a safe distance from the blue helmet, they stopped, and the large boy handed William his cap.

"Ere you *are*," he said, with a certain respect.

William, with a careless gesture, tossed the cap into the air. "Don't want it," he said.

"Wot's yer nime?"

"William."

"'E's called Bill," said the boy to the others.

William read in their faces a growing interest, not quite friendship yet, but still not quite contempt. He glowed with pride. He put his hands into the pockets of his overcoat and there met—a sixpence—joy!

"Wot's your name?" he said to his late adversary.

"'Erb," said the other, still staring at William with interest.

"Come on, 'Erb," said William jauntily, "let's buy

some sweets, eh?"

He entered a small, unsavoury sweetshop, and the whole tribe crowded in after him. He and 'Erb discussed the rival merits of bulls' eyes and cokernut kisses at length.

"Them larses longer," said 'Erb, "but these 'ere tases nicer."

Finally, William airily tasted one of the cokernut kisses and the whole tribe followed his example—to be chased by the indignant shopkeeper all the way down the street.

"*Eatin*' of 'em!" he shouted furiously. "*Eatin*' of 'em without *payin*' for 'em. I'll set the cops on ye—ye young thieves."

* * *

They rushed along the next street shouting, whistling and pushing each other. William's whistle was louder than any, he ran the foremost. The lust of lawlessness was growing on him. They swarmed in at the next sweetshop, and William purchased sixpennyworth of bulls' eyes and poured them recklessly out of the bag into the grimy, outstretched palms that surrounded him.

William had no idea where he was. His hands were as grimy as the hands of his companions, his face was streaked with dirt wherever his hands had touched it, his eye was black, his collar was gone, his hair was wild, his overcoat had lost its look of tailored freshness. And he was happy at last.

He was no longer a little gentleman staying at a select hotel with his family. He was a boy among boys—an outlaw among outlaws once more. He was no longer a pariah. He had proved his valour in fighting and running and whistling. He was almost accepted, not

WILLIAM WAS HAPPY AT LAST. HE WAS A BOY AMONG
BOYS—AN OUTLAW AMONG OUTLAWS.

THEY RUSHED ALONG THE NEXT STREET, SHOUTING AND WHISTLING.

quite. He was alight with exhilaration.

In the next street a watering cart had just passed, and there was a broad muddy stream flowing along the gutter. With a whoop of joy the tribe made for it, 'Erb at the head, closely followed by William.

William's patent leather shoes began to lose their, damning smartness. It was William who began to stamp as he walked, and the rest at once followed suit—splashing, shouting, whistling, jostling, they followed the muddy stream through street after street. At every corner William seemed to shed yet another portion of the nice equipment of the boy-who-is-going-to-a-party. No party would have claimed him now—no hostess greeted him—no housemaid admitted him—he had completely "burned his boats." But he was happy.

All good things come to an end, however, even a muddy stream in a gutter, and 'Erb, still leader, called out: "Come on, you chaps! Come on, Bill—bells!"

Along both sides of a street they flew at break-neck speed, pulling every bell as they passed. Three enraged householders pursued them. One of them, fleeter than the other two, caught the smallest and slowest of the tribe and began to execute corporal punishment.

It was William who returned, charged from behind, left the householder winded in the gutter, and dragged the yelling scapegoat to the shelter of his tribe.

"Good ole Bill," said 'Erb, and William's heart swelled again with pride. Nothing on earth would now have checked his victorious career.

A motor-van passed with another gang of street-urchins hanging on merrily behind. With a yell of battle, William hurled himself upon them, struggled with them in mid-air, and established himself, cheering on his own tribe and pushing off the others.

In the fight William lost his overcoat, his Eton coat was torn from top to bottom, and his waistcoat ripped open. But his tribe won the day; the rival tribe dropped off, hurling ineffectual taunts and insults, and on sailed William and his gang, half-running, half-riding, with an exhilarating mixture of physical exercise and joy-riding unknown to the more law-abiding citizen.

And in the midst was William—William serene and triumphant, William dirty and ragged, William acclaimed leader at last. The motor-van put on speed. There was a ride of pure breathless joy and peril before, at last exhausted, they dropped off.

*   *   *

Then 'Erb turned to William: "Wot you doin' tonight, maite?" he said.

"Maite!" William's heart glowed.

"Nothin', maite," answered William carelessly.

"Oi'm goin' to the picshers," said 'Erb. "If you loike ter help my o'd woman with the corfee-stall, she'll give yer a tanner."

A coffee-stall—Oh, joy! Was the magic of this evening inexhaustible?

"Oi'll 'elp 'er orl *roight*, maite," said William, making an effort to acquire his new friend's accent and intonation.

"Oi'll taike yer near up to it," said 'Erb, and to the gang: "Nah, you run orf 'ome, kids. Me an' Bill is busy."

He gave William a piece of chewing-gum, which William proudly took and chewed and swallowed, and led him to a street-corner, from where a coffee-stall could be seen in a glare of flaming oil-jets.

"You just say ''Erb sent me,' an' you bet you'll get a tanner when she shuts up—if she's not in a paddy. Go on. Goo'-night."

He fled, leaving William to approach the stall alone. A large, untidy woman regarded him with arms akimbo.

"I've come ter' elp with the stall," said William, trying to speak with the purest of Cockney accents. "'Erb sent me."

The woman regarded him with a hostile stare, still with arms akimbo.

"Oh, 'e did, did 'e? 'E's allus ready ter send someone else. 'E's gone ter the picshers, I suppose? 'E's a nice son for a poor woman ter 'ave, isn't 'e? Larkin' abaht orl day an' goin' ter picshers orl night—an' where do *Oi* come in? I asks yer, where do *Oi* come in?"

William, feeling that some reply was expected, said that he didn't know. She looked him up and down. Her expression implied that her conclusions were far from complimentary.

"An' *you*—I serpose—one of the young divvils 'e picks up from 'Evving knows where. Told yer yer'd git a tanner, I serpose? Well, yer'll git a tanner if yer be'aves ter *my* likin', an' yer'll git a box on the ears if yer don'. Oh, come on, do; don't stand there orl night. 'Ere's the hapron—buns is a penny each, an' sangwiches a penny each, and cups o' corfy a penny each. Git a move on."

He was actually installed behind the counter. He was actually covered from neck to foot in a white apron. His rapture knew no bounds. He served strong men with sandwiches and cups of coffee. He dropped their pennies into the wooden till. He gave change (generally wrong). He turned the handle of the fascinating urn. He could not resist the handle of the little urn. When there were no customers he turned the handle, to see the little brown stream gush out in little spurts on to the floor or on to the counter.

His feeling of importance as he handed over buns and received pennies was indescribable. He felt like a king—like a god. He had forgotten all about his family . . .

Then the stout lady presented him with a bowl of hot water, a dish-cloth, and a towel, and told him to wash up. Wash up! He had never washed up before. He swished the water round the bowl with the dishcloth very fast one way, and then quickly changed and swished it round the other. It was fascinating. He lifted the dish-cloth high out of the water and swirled the thin stream to and fro. He soaked his apron and swamped the floor.

Finally, his patroness, who had been indulging in a doze, awoke and fixed eyes of horror upon him.

"What yer think yer a-doing of?" she said indignantly.

"Yer think yer at the seaside, don't yer? Yer think yer've got yer little bucket an' spade, don't yer? Waistin' of good water—spoilin' of a good hapron. Where did 'Erb find *yer*, I'd like ter know. Picked yer aht of a lunatic asylum, *I* should say . . . Oh, lumme, 'ere's toffs comin'. Sharp, now, be ready wiv the hurn an' try an' 'ave a *bit* of sense, an' heverythin' double price fer toffs, now—don't forget."

* * *

But William, with a sinking heart, had recognised the toffs. Looking wildly round he saw a large cap (presumably 'Erb's) on a lower shelf of the stall. He seized it, put it on, and dragged it over his eyes. The "toffs" approached—four of them. One of them, the elder lady, seemed upset.

"Have you seen," she said to the owner of the stall, "a little boy anywhere about—a little boy in an Eton suit?"

"No, mam," said the proprietress, "I hain't seen no one in a heton suit."

"He was going out to a party," went on Mrs. Brown breathlessly, "and he must have got lost on the way. They rang up to say he hadn't arrived, and the police have had no news of him, and we've traced him to this locality. You—you haven't seen a little boy that looked as if he were going to a party?"

"No, mam," said the lady of the coffee-stall. "I hain't seen no little boy goin' to no party this hevening."

"Oh, mother," said Ethel; and William, trying to hide his face between his cap-brim and his apron, groaned in spirit as he heard her voice. "Do let's have some coffee now we're here."

"Very well, darling," said Mrs. Brown. "Four cups of coffee, please."

William, still cowering under his cap, poured them

out and handed them over the counter.

"You couldn't mistake him," said Mrs. Brown tearfully. "He had a nice blue overcoat over his Eton suit, and a blue cap to match, and patent leather shoes, and he was *so* looking forward to the party, I can't think——"

"How much?" said William's father to William.

"Twopence each," muttered William.

There was a horrible silence.

"I beg your pardon," said William's father suavely, and William's heart sank.

"Twopence each," he muttered again.

There was another horrible silence.

"May I trouble you," went on William's father—and from the deadly politeness of his tone, William realised that all was over—"may I trouble you to remove your cap a moment? Something about your voice and the lower portion of your face reminds me of a near relative of mine——"

But it was Robert who snatched 'Erb's cap from his head and stripped his apron from him, and said: "You young devil!" and Ethel who said: "Goodness, just *look* at his clothes," and Mrs. Brown who said: "Oh, my darling little William, and I thought I'd lost you"; and the lady of the coffee-stall who said: "Well, yer can *'ave* 'im fer all 'e knows abaht washin' up."

And William returned sad but unrepentant to the bosom of outraged Respectability.

Chapter 8

William Advertises

A new sweetshop, Mallards by name, had been opened in the village. It had been the sensation of the week to William and his friends. For it sold everything a halfpenny cheaper than Mr. Moss.

It revolutionised the finances of the Outlaws. The Outlaws was the secret society which comprised William and his friends, Ginger, Henry, and Douglas. Jumble, William's disreputable mongrel, was its mascot.

The Outlaws patronised Mallards generously on the first Saturday of its career. William spent his whole threepence there on separate halfpennyworths. He insisted on the halfpennyworths. He said firmly that Mr. Moss always let him have halfpennyworths. In the end the red-haired young woman behind the counter yielded to him. She yielded reluctantly and scornfully. She took no interest in his choice. She asked him in a voice of bored contempt not to finger the Edinburgh Rock. She muttered as she did up his package—"waste of paper and time"—"never heard such nonsense"—"ha'porths *indeed.*"

William went out of the shop, placing his five minute packets in already over-full pockets and keeping out the sixth for present consumption.

"I'm not *sure,*" he said darkly to Ginger and Henry, who accompanied him—Douglas was away from

home—"I'm not *sure* as I'm ever going *there* again——
Have a bull's eye?—I didn't like the way she looked at
me nor spoke at me—an' I've a jolly *good* mind not to go
to Mallards next Saturday."

"But it's cheap," said Ginger, taking out his package.
"Have an aniseed ball?—an' it's *cheap* that matters in a
shop, I should think."

"Well, I don't *know*," said William, with an air of
wisdom. "That's all I say—I jus' don't *know*—I jus'
don't *know* that cheap's all that matters."

"Well, wot else matters? You tell me that," said
Henry, crunching up a bull's eye and an aniseed ball
simultaneously, and taking out his package. "Have a
pear drop?—You jus' tell me wot matters besides *cheap*
in a shop."

William, perceiving that the general feeling was
against him, put another bull's eye in his mouth and
waxed irritable.

"Well, don't talk about it so much," he said. "You
keep talkin' an' talkin'——" Then an argument occurred to him, and he brought it out with triumph. "S'pose
anyone was a *murderer*—well, wot would cheap have to
do with it?—S'pose someone wot had a shop murdered
someone—well, I s'pose if they was *cheap* you'd say it
was all right! Huh!"

With an expression of intense scorn and amusement
William put the last bull's eye into his mouth, threw
away the paper, and took out the treacle toffee.

"Well, who's she murdered?" said Ginger pugnaciously. "Jus' 'cause she din' want to give you ha'porths
you go an' say she's *murdered* someone. Well, who's
she murdered, that's all?—you can't go callin' folks
murderers an' not prove *who* they've murdered. Bring
out *who* she's murdered—that's all."

William was at the moment deeply engrossed in his

treacle toffee.

The red-haired girl had given it an insufficient allowance of paper, and in William's pocket it had lost even this, and formed a deep attachment to a piece of putty which a friendly plumber had kindly given him the day before. The piece of putty was at that moment the apple of William's eye. He detached it gently from the toffee and examined it tenderly to make sure that it was not harmed. Finally he replaced it in his pocket and put the toffee in his mouth. Then he returned to the argument.

"How can I bring out who she's murdered if she's murdered them. That's a sens'ble thing to say, isn't it? If she's *murdered* 'em she's *buried* 'em. Do you think folks wot murder folks leaves 'em about for other folks to bring out to show they've murdered 'em? You've not got much sense. That's all I say. You don't know much about *murderers*. Why do you keep talkin' about murderers if you don't know anything about 'em?"

Ginger was growing slightly bewildered. Arguments with William often left him bewildered. He was inclined, on the whole, to think that perhaps William was right, and she had murdered someone.

At this point Jumble created a diversion. Jumble loved treacle toffee, and he had caught a whiff of the divine perfume. He sat up promptly to beg for some, but the Outlaws' mascot was seldom lucky himself. He sat up on the very edge of a ditch, and William could not resist giving him a push.

Jumble picked himself out of the bottom of the ditch and shook off the water, grinning and wagging his tail. Jumble was a sportsman. William had finished the treacle toffee, but Henry threw Jumble an aniseed ball, which he licked, rolled with his paw, and abandoned, and which Henry then carefully put back with the others

in his packet. Then William threw a stick for him, and
the discussion of the red-haired girl's morals was
definitely abandoned.

*　　　*　　　*

At the corner of the road they espied Joan Crewe.
Though fluffy and curled and exquisitely dressed
herself, Joan adored William's roughness and untidi-
ness.

"Hello!" said Joan.

"Hello!" said the Outlaws.

"Have you been to Mallards'?" said Joan.

"Umph!" said the Outlaws.

"It's a halfpenny cheaper than Moss'."

"Yes," said Ginger, "but William says she's a
murderer."

"I *di'n't*," said William irritably. "You can't understand English. That's wot wrong with you. You can't
understand English. Wot I said *was*——"

Finding that he had entirely forgotten how the
argument arose, he hastily changed the subject. "Wot
you're goin' to do now?" he said.

"Anything," said Joan obligingly.

"Have a cocoa-nut lump?" said William, taking out
his third bag.

"Have an aniseed ball?" said Ginger.

"Have a pear drop?" said Henry.

Joan took one of each and took out a bag from her
pocket.

"Have a liquorice treasure?" she said.

Munching cheerfully they walked along the road,
stopping to throw a stick for Jumble every now and then.
Jumble then performed his "trick." His "trick" was to
walk between William and Ginger, a paw in each of their

hands. It was a "trick" that Jumble cordially detested.
He generally managed to avoid it. The word "trick"
generally sent him flying towards the horizon like an
arrow from a bow. But this time he was hoping that
William still had some treacle toffee concealed on his
person, and did not take to his heels in time. He was
finally released with a kiss from Joan on the end of his
nose. In joy at his freedom, he found a stick, worried it,
ran after his tail, and finally darted down the road.

"Have a monkey-nut?" said William.

They partook of his last packet.

"I once heard a boy say," said Henry solemnly, "that
people who eat monkey-nuts get monkey puzzle trees
growin' out of their mouths."

"I don't s'pose," said Ginger, as he swallowed his,
"that jus' a few could do it."

"Anyway, it would be rather interestin'," said
William, "going about with a tree comin' out of your
mouth—you could slash things about with it."

"But think of the orful pain," said Henry dejectedly;
"roots growin' inside your stomach."

Joan handed her monkey-nut back to William.

"I—I don't think I'll have one, thank you, William,"
she said.

"All right," said William, philosophically cracking it
and putting it into his mouth. "I don't mind eatin' 'em.
Let 'em start growin' trees out of *my* stomach if they
can."

They were nearing a little old-fashioned sweetshop. A
man in check trousers, shirt-sleeves, and a white apron
stood in the doorway. Generally Mr. Moss radiated
cheerfulness. To-day he looked depressed. They
approached him somewhat guiltily.

"Well," he said. "You coming to spend your Saturday
money?"

"Er–no," said William.

"We've spent it," said Ginger.

"At Mallards'," said Henry.

"It's—it's a halfpenny cheaper," said Joan.

"Well," said Mr. Moss, "I don't blame you. Mind, I don't blame you. You're quite right to go where it's a halfpenny cheaper. You'd be foolish if you didn't go where it's a halfpenny cheaper. But all I say is it's not fair on me. They're a big company, they are, and I'm not. They've got shops all over the big towns, they have, and I've not. They've got capital behind 'em, they have, and I've not. They can afford to give things away, an' I can't. I've always kept prices as low as I could so as jus' to be able to keep myself on 'em, an' I can't lower them no further. That's where they've got me. They can undercut. They don't need to make a profit at first. An' all I say is it's not fair on me. They say as this here place is growin' an' there's room for the two of us. Well, all I can say is not more'n ten people's come into this here shop since they set up, an' it's not fair on me."

His audience of four, clustered around his shop-door, listened in big-eyed admiration. As he stopped for breath, William said earnestly:

"Well, we won't buy no *more* of their ole stuff, anyway——"

The Outlaws confirmed this statement eagerly, but Mr. Moss raised his hand. "No," he said. "You oughter go where you get stuff cheapest. I don't blame you. You're quite right."

They walked along in silence for a little while. The memory of Mr. Moss, wistful and bewildered, with his cheerful hilarity gone, remained with them.

"I won't go to that Old Mallards' again while I live," said William firmly.

"Anyway, she wasn't nice. I didn't like her," said Joan.

"She didn't *care* what you bought?" said William indignantly. "She didn't take any *interest* like wot Mr. Moss does."

"Yes, an' if she *murders* folks as William says she does——" began Ginger.

"I wish you'd shut *up* talking about that," said William. "I di'n't say she'd murdered anyone."

"You did."

"I di'n't."

"You *did*."

"I *di'n't*."

"Do have another liquorice treasure," said Joan.

Peaceful munchings were resumed.

"Anyway," said William, returning to the matter in hand, "I'd like to *do* something for Mr. Moss."

"Wot *could* we do?" said Ginger.

"We could stop folks goin' to old Mallards'—'Tisn't as if she took any *int*'rest in wot you buy."

"Well, *how* could we stop folks goin' to ole Mallards'?"

"*Make* 'em go to Mr. Moss."

"Well, *how*—why don't you say *how*?"

"Well, we'd have to have a meeting about it—an Outlaw meeting. Let's have one now. Let's go to our woodshed an' have one now."

Joan's face fell.

"I can't come, can I? I'm not an Outlaw."

"You can be an Outlaw ally," said William kindly. "We'll make up a special oath for you, an' give you a special secret sign."

Joan's eyes shone.

"Oh, thank you, William darling."

*   *   *

Joan had taken the special oath. It had consisted of the words: "I will not betray the secrets of the Outlaws, an' I will stick up for the Outlaws till death do us part."

The last phrase was an inspiration of Henry's, who had been to his cousin's wedding the week before.

They sat down on logs or stacks of firewood or packing-cases to consider the question of Mr. Moss.

"First thing is," said William, with a business-like frown, "we've got to make people go to Mr. Moss."

"Well, how can we?" objected Ginger. "Jus' tell me that? How can we make people go to Moss' when Mallards' is halfpenny cheaper?"

"Same way as big shops make people go to them— they put up notices an' things—they say their things is better than other shops' things, an' folks believes 'em."

"Well, why should folks believe 'em?" said Ginger pugnaciously. Henry was engaged upon his last few pear drops and had no time for conversation. "Why should folks b'lieve 'em when they say they're better than other shops? An' how can we stick up notices an' where an' who'll let us stick up notices? You don't talk sense. You're mad, that's wot you are. First you go about calling folks murderers when you don't know *who* they've murdered, nor nothin' about it, an' then you talk about stickin' up notices when there isn't anyone who'd let us stick up any notices, nor anyone who'd take any notice of notices wot we stuck up nor——"

"If you'd jus' stop talkin'," said William, "an' deafenin' us all for jus' a bit. You've been talkin' an' deafenin' us all ever since you came out. D'you think we never want to hear anythin' all our lives ever till death, but you talkin' an' deafenin' us all? There *is* things that we'd like to hear 'sides you talkin' an' deafenin' us all—there's music an' birds singing, an'—an' other folks talkin', but you go on so's anyone would think that——"

Here Ginger hurled himself upon William, and the
two of them rolled on to the floor and wrestled among
the faggots. Violent physical encounters were a regular
part of the programme of the Outlaws' meetings. Henry
watched nonchalantly from his perch, crunching pear
drops, occasionally throwing small twigs at them, and
saying: "Go it!"—"That's right!"—"Go *it!*" Joan
watched with anxious horror, and "William, do be
careful," and: "Oh, Ginger, darling, don't hurt him."

Finally the combatants rose, dusty and dishevelled,
shook hands, and resumed their seats on the stacks of
firewood.

"Now, if you'll only let me *speak*——" began
William.

"We will, William, darling," said Joan. "Ginger
won't interrupt, will you, Ginger?"

Ginger, who had decidedly had the worst of the
battle, was removing dust and twigs from his mouth. He
gave a non-committal grunt.

"Well, you know the Sale of Work next week?" went
on William. They groaned. It was a ceremony to which
each of the company would be led, brushed and combed
and dressed in gala clothes, in a proud parent's wake.

"Well," went on William. "You jus' listen carefully. I
got an idea."

They leant forward eagerly. They had a touching faith
in William's ideas that no amount of bitter experiences
seemed able to destroy.

*   *   *

The day of the Sale of Work was warm and cloudless.
William's mother and sister worked there all the
morning. A tent had been erected, and inside the tent
were a few select stalls of flowers and vegetables.

Outside on the grass were the other stalls. The opening ceremony was to be performed by a real live duke.

William absented himself for the greater part of the morning, returning in time for lunch, and meekly offering himself to be cleaned and dressed afterwards like the proverbial lamb for the slaughter.

"William," said Mrs. Brown to her husband, "is being almost too good to be true. It's such a comfort."

"I'm glad you can take comfort in it," said Mr. Brown. "From my knowledge of William, I prefer him when you know what tricks he's up to."

"Oh, I think you misjudge him," said Mrs. Brown, whose trust in William was almost pathetic.

"Ethel and I can't go to the opening, darling," said Mrs. Brown at lunch. "I'm rather tired. So I suppose you'll wait and go with us later."

William smiled his painfully sweet smile.

"I might as well go early. I might be able to help someone," he said shamelessly.

Half an hour later William set off alone to the Sale of Work. He wore his super-best clothes. His hair was brushed to a chastened, sleek smoothness. He wore kid gloves. His shoes shone like stars.

He walked briskly down to the Sale of Work. Already a gay throng had assembled there. Joan was there, looking like a piece of thistledown in fluffy white, with her mother. Ginger was there, stiff and immaculate, with his mother.

William, Ginger, and Henry joined forces and stood talking in low, conspiratorial voices, looking rather uncomfortable in their excessive cleanness. Joan looked at them wistfully but was kept close to the maternal side.

The real live duke arrived. He was tall and stooping, and looked very bored and aristocratic.

Everything was ready for the opening. It was to take

place on the open space of grass at the back of the tent. The chairs for the committee and the chair for the duke were close to the tent. Then a space was railed off from the crowd—from the ordinary people.

At the other side of the tent the stalls were deserted. His Grace stood for a few minutes in the tent by one of the stalls talking to the vicar's wife. Then he went out to open the Sale of Work. A few minutes after his Grace had departed, William might have been seen to emerge from beneath the stall, his cap gone, his hair deranged, his knees dusty, and join Ginger and Henry in the deserted space behind the tent.

His Grace stood and uttered the few languid words that declared the Sale of Work open. But the committee who were a few yards behind him sat in open-mouthed astonishment. For a large placard adorned his Grace's coat behind.

> HAVE YOU TRYD
> MOSSES
> COKERNUT LUMPS?

The committee could think of no course of action with which to meet this crisis. They could only gasp with horror, open-eyed and open-mouthed.

The few gracious words were said. The applause rose. His Grace turned round to converse pleasantly with the Vicar's wife, exposing his back to the view of the crowd. The applause wavered, then redoubled ecstatically.

"Some kind of an advertising job," said the organist's wife.

But the crowd did not mind what it was. They held their sides. They clung to each other in helpless mirth. They followed that tall, slim, elegant figure with its incongruous placard as it went with the vicar's wife round the tent to the stalls. The vicar's wife talked nervously and hysterically. "My dear, I *couldn't*," she said afterwards. "I didn't know how to put it. I couldn't think of words—and I kept thinking, suppose he knows

HIS GRACE EXAMINED THE PLACARD, THEN TURNED TO THE VICAR. "HOW LONG EXACTLY," HE SAID SLOWLY, "HAVE I BEEN WEARING THIS?"

and *means* it to be there. It somehow seemed better bred to ignore it."

The committee clustered together in an anxious group.

"It wasn't there when he came. Someone must have put it on."

"My dear, someone must tell him."

"Or creep up and take it off when he isn't looking."

"My dear—one couldn't. Suppose he turned round when one was doing it, and thought one was putting it *on!*"

"The vicar must tell him—let's find the vicar. I think it would come better from a clergyman, don't you?"

"Yes, and he might —well, he couldn't say much before a clergyman, could he?"

"And a vicar is so practised in consolation. I think you're right—— But who did it?"

Flustered, panting, distraught, they hastened off in search of the vicar.

AT THAT MOMENT, WILLIAM, GINGER AND HENRY EMERGED FROM BENEATH ONE OF THE STALLS.

* * *

Meanwhile, his Grace talked to the

vicar's wife. He was beginning to think that she was not quite herself. Her manner seemed more than peculiar. He glanced round. The stalls were still deserted.

"They haven't begun to buy much yet, have they?" he said. "I suppose I must set the example."

He wandered over to a stall and bought a pink cushion. Then he looked around again, his cushion under his arm, his placard still adorning the back of his coat. The crowd were engaged only in staring at him; they were fighting to get a glimpse of him; they were following him about like dogs——

"I suppose some of these people must know my name," he said. "I thought that speech of mine in the House last week would wake people up——"

"Er—Oh, yes," said the vicar's wife. She blinked and swallowed. "Er—Oh, yes—indeed, yes—indeed, yes—I quite agree—er—quite!"

Here the vicar rescued her.

The vicar had not quite made up his mind whether to be jocular or condoling.

"A splendid attendance, isn't it, your Grace? There's a little thing I want to——" The vicar's wife tactfully glided away. "Of course we all understand—you're not responsible—and, on our honour, we aren't—quite an accident—the guilty party, however, shall be found. I assure you he shall—er—shall be found."

"Would you mind," said his Grace patiently, "telling me of what you are talking?"

The vicar drew a deep breath, then took the plunge.

"There's a small placard on your back," he said. "Well, not small—that is—allow me——"

His Grace hastily felt behind, secured the placard, tore it off, put on his tortoise-shell spectacles, and examined it at arm's length. Then he turned to the vicar,

who was mopping his brow. The committee were
trembling in the background. One of them—Miss
Spence by name—had already succumbed to a nervous
breakdown and had had to go home. Another was
having hysterics in the tent.

"How long exactly," asked his Grace slowly, "have I
been wearing this?"

The vicar smiled mirthlessly, and put up a hand
nervously as if to loosen his collar.

"Er–quite a matter of minutes—ahem—of minutes
one might say, your Grace, since—ah—ahem—since
the opening, one might almost put it——"

"Then," said his Grace, "why the devil didn't you tell
me before?"

The vicar put up his hand and coughed reproachfully.

At this moment William, Ginger and Henry emerged
from beneath one of the stalls, in whose butter-muslined
shelter they had been preparing themselves, and
awaiting the most dramatic moment to appear.

They all wore "sandwiches" made from sheets of
cardboard and joined over their shoulders by string.

William bore   —and behind
before him—   him

MOSSES TREEKLE TOFFY IS THE BEST	GET YOUR BULLS EYES AT MOSSES

Ginger bore   —and behind
before him–   him

```
┌─────────────────┐    ┌─────────────────┐
│    YOU WILL     │    │     MOSSES      │
│     LIKE        │    │     TAKES       │
│    MOSSES       │    │       AN        │
│    MUNKY        │    │   INTEREST      │
│     NUTS        │    │                 │
└─────────────────┘    └─────────────────┘
```

Henry bore   —and behind
before him—   him

```
┌─────────────────┐    ┌─────────────────┐
│  GO TO MOSSES   │    │     MOSSES      │
│      FOR        │    │                 │
│    FRUTY        │    │     MAKES       │
│     BITS        │    │                 │
│                 │    │    HAPOTHS      │
└─────────────────┘    └─────────────────┘
```

Solemnly, with expressionless faces and eyes fixed in front of them, they paraded through the crowd. His Grace, who had taken off his spectacles, put them on again. His Grace was a good judge of faces.

"Secure that first boy," he said.

The vicar, nothing loth, secured William by the collar and brought him before his Grace. His Grace held out his placard.

"Did you—er—attach this to my coat?" he asked sternly.

William shook off the vicar's hand.

"Yes," he said, as sternly as his Grace. "You see, we wanted people to go to Mr. Moss' shop—'cause, you

see, Mallards' is a big company, an' he's not, an' they've
got—er—capitols behind them and he's not—see? And
we wanted to make people go to Moss', and we thought
we'd fix up notices wot'd *make* people go to Moss' like
big shops do—an' we knew no one'd take any notice of
our notices if we jus' put 'em up anywhere, but we
thought if we fixed one on to someone important wot
everyone'd be lookin' at all the time—an' he's awful
kind an' he takes an' *int'rest* an' he *cares* wot you get an'
his cokernut lumps is better'n anyone's, an' he makes
ha'p'oths without makin' a fuss—an' he's awful *worried*,
an' we wanted to help him——"

"An' *she's* a murderer," piped Ginger.

Before his Grace could reply Joan wrenched herself
free from her mother's restraining hand and flew up to
the group.

"Oh, please *don't* do anything to William," she
pleaded. "It was my fault, too—I'm not a real one, but
I'm an ally—till death do us part, you know."

His Grace looked from one to the other. He had been
bored almost to tears by the vicar's wife and the
committee. With a lightening of the heart he recognised
more entertaining company.

"Well," he said judicially, "come to the refreshment
tent and we'll talk it over, over an ice."

* * *

The news that his Grace had spent almost the entire
afternoon eating ices with William Brown and those
other children, discussing pirates and Red Indians, and
telling them stories of big game hunting, made the
village gasp.

The further knowledge that he had asked them to
walk down to the station with him, had called at Moss',
tasted cokernut lumps, pronounced them delicious,

bought a pound for each of them, and ordered a monthly supply, left the village almost paralysed. But everyone went to Mr. Moss' to ask for details. Mr. Moss was known as the confectioner who supplied the Duke of Ashbridge with cokernut lumps. Mallards' shop was let to a baker's the next month, and the red-haired girl said that *she* wasn't sorry—of all the dead-and-alive holes to work in this place was the deadest.

It was Miss Spence who voiced the prevailing sentiment about William. She did not say it out of affection for William. She had no affection for William.

William chased her cat and her hens, disturbed her rest with his unearthly songs and whistles, broke her windows with his cricket ball, and threw stones over the hedge into her garden pond.

But one day, as she watched William progress along the ditch—William never walked on the road if he could walk in the ditch—dragging his toes in the mud, his hands in his pockets, his head poking forward, his brows frowning, his freckled face stern and determined, his mouth pucked up to make his devastating whistle, his train of boy followers behind him, she said slowly: "There's something *about* that boy——"

Chapter 9

William and the Black Cat

Bunker, the old black cat, had been an inhabitant of William's home ever since he could remember. Bunker officially belonged to Ethel, William's sister, but he bestowed his presence impartially on every family in the neighbourhood. He frequently haunted the next door garden, where lived another black cat, a petted darling named Luke, belonging to Miss Amelia Blake.

William treated all cats with supreme contempt. Towards his own family's cat he unbent occasionally so far as to throw twigs at it or experiment upon it with pots of coloured paints, but he prided himself upon despising cats, and considered that their only use in the world was to give exercise and pleasure to his beloved mongrel, Jumble.

When William lay in bed and Miss Amelia Blake's tender accents rose nightly to his ears from the next garden, "Luky, Luky, Luky, Luky, Luk-ee-ee-*ee!*" he would frown scornfully.

"Huh! All for an ole *cat!* Fancy *knowin'* 'em."

His boast was that he did not know one cat from another.

Bunker was very old and very mangy. He employed habitually an ear-splitting and horrible yell, long drawn out and increasing in volume as it neared its nightmare climax—a yell which William loved to imitate.

"Yah-ah-ah-ah-ah-Ah-AH!"

Mr. Brown remarked many times that that cat and that boy would drive him to drink between them, but at least that boy slept at night. It was decided one morning, when Bunker had spent a whole night in the garden without once relaxing the efforts of his vocal chords, that Bunker should leave this unsympathetic world for some sphere where, one hoped, his voice could be better appreciated, or, at any rate, submitted to some tuning process.

"Well, he goes, or I go," said Mr. Brown. "One or other of us must be destroyed. The world can't hold us both. You can take your choice."

Thus Bunker's fate was sealed.

Ethel, who had hardly looked at Bunker for months without disgust, began, now that his dissolution was imminent, to dwell upon his engaging kittenhood, to see him in her mind's eye as a black ball with a blue ribbon around his neck, and to experience all the feelings that one ought to experience when one's beloved pet is torn from one by Death. She would even have fondled him if he hadn't been so mangy. When his hideous voice upraised itself she would murmur, "My darling Bunker." And only a week ago she had murmured, "Why we *keep* that cat, I can't think."

One afternoon when Ethel was at the tennis club, Mrs. Brown approached William mysteriously.

"William, dear, I think it would be so kind of you to take Bunker to Gorton's now while Ethel is out. I've told Mr. Gorton and he's expecting him, and it would be much nicer for Ethel just to hear that it was all over."

Nothing loth to help in Bunker's destruction, William took the covered basket from the pantry and went into the garden, caught a glimpse of black fur beyond the summer-house, crept up behind it, grabbed it with a triumphant "Would you?" and clapped it into the basket.

*　　*　　*

Gorton's was a wonderland to William—dogs in cages, cats in cages, guinea-pigs in cages, rabbits in cages, white rats in cages, tortoises in cages, gold-fish in bowls.

Once William had been thrilled to see a monkey there. William had stood outside the shop for a whole morning watching it and making encouraging conciliatory noises to it which it answered by an occasional jabber that delighted William's very soul. William was glad of an errand that gave him an excuse for wandering round the fascinations of the shop. He handed his basket to Mr. Gorton, and began his tour of inspection. He spent half an hour in front of the cage of a parrot, who screamed repeatedly, "Go—*away*, you ass, go *away!*"

William would never have tired of the joy of listening to this, but, discovering that it was almost tea-time, he reluctantly took up his empty basket and returned.

When he entered the dining-room, Mrs. Brown was speaking to Ethel.

"Ethel, darling, William very kindly took dear Bunker to Mr. Gorton's this afternoon. We wanted you to be spared the pain of knowing till it was over, but now it's over and Bunker didn't suffer at all, you know, darling, and——"

At that moment there arose from the garden the familiar hair-raising, ear-splitting sound. "Yah-ah-ah-ah-AH!"

Ethel burst into tears.

"It's Bunker's ghost," she said. "Oh, it's his ghost."

But it wasn't Bunker's ghost, for Bunker's solid, earthly, mangy form appeared at that very moment upon the window-sill.

William's heart stood still. In the sudden silence that greeted the apparition of the earthly body of Bunker, his mind grasped the important fact that he must have taken the wrong cat, and that the less he said about it the better.

"William," said Mrs. Brown reproachfully, "you might have done a little thing like that for your sister."

"I thought——" said William feebly, "I mean, I meant——"

"Well, you must do it after tea," said Mrs. Brown firmly; "it isn't kind of you to cause your sister all this unnecessary suffering just because you're too lazy to walk down to Gorton's."

His sister, who was finding it difficult to whip up a loving sorrow for Bunker, while Bunker, mangy and alive, stared at her through the window, said nothing and William muttered: "All right—after tea—I'll go after tea."

He went after tea. He handed the basket to Mr. Gorton with an unblushing: "There was two really to be done—here's the other."

He stood oppressed by the thought of his crime, and waited the return of his basket. He had even lost interest in Mr. Gorton's wonderland. When the parrot screamed, "Go *away*, you ass, go *away*," he replied huffily, "Go away yourself."

As he lay in bed that night, he wondered vaguely whose cat he had consigned to an untimely death.

He soon knew.

"Luky, Luky, Luky, Luky, Luk-ee-ee-*ee*. Where are you, darling? Luky?—Luky? Luky, Luky, Luky, Luky, Luky, Lukee-ee-ee-*ee*? What's happened to you, Luky?

Where are you, darling? Luky, Luky, Luky, Luky, Luk-ee-ee-ee-*ee*."

It seemed to William to go on all night.

*   *   *

William's excursions in the character of robber chief, outlaw, or Red Indian, took him many miles outside the radius of his own village. Three days after the day of his ill-omened mistake he was passing a wayside cottage (in the character of a famous detective on the track of crime), when he noticed a large black cat sitting upon the doorstep washing its face. There was something familiar about that cat. William stopped. It wasn't Bunker, but was it——

"Luky," said William in a hoarse persuasive whisper.

The large black cat rose purring and came down the walk to William.

"Luky," said William again.

The large black cat rubbed itself fondly against William's boots.

A woman came out of the cottage smiling.

"You admirin' my pussy, little boy?"

In ordinary circumstances, William would have resented most bitterly this mode of address and would have passed on with a silent glance of contempt. But from William's heart the load of murder had been lifted. He almost smiled.

"Umph!" he said.

"He *is* a nice pussy, isn't he?" went on Luky's new owner. "I bought him at Gorton's, three days ago. He was just what I wanted—a nice full-grown cat. Kittens are so destructive. He's called Twinkie. Twinkie, Twinkie, Twinkie," she murmured fondly bending down to stroke him, her voice rising affectionately in the scale at each repetition of his name.

Luky rubbed himself purring against her boots.

"There!" she said proudly, "don't the dear dumb creature know its new mistress . . . There then, darling. You come in an' see the beauty lap up its milk some time, little boy, and I'll give you a ginger-bread. I like little boys to be fond of animals—especially cats. Some nasty boys throw sticks and things at them, but I'm quite sure you wouldn't, would you?"

William muttered something inaudible and set off down the road, his heart torn between relief at knowing himself guiltless of the crime of murder and indignant shame at being accused of an affection for cats—*cats!* But he was horrified at the duplicity of Mr. Gorton, and decided to confront him with it at once. He hastened to the cage-hung shop and, spending only ten minutes in front of the box of grass snakes, entered the cool, dark depths where Mr. Gorton, in his shirt sleeves, was chewing tobacco.

Mr. Gorton was a large, burly man with a fat, good-natured-looking face, and a gentle manner. But Mr. Gorton obeyed the Scriptures in combining with his dove-like gentleness a serpent-like cunning.

"Now look 'ere, young gent," he said, when William had laid his accusation before him. "You say I sold that there hanimal. Now wot you wanted was to be rid of that hanimal, didn't you? Well, you're rid of it, haren't you? So wot've you got to grumble at? See? 'As that there hanimal come back to trouble you? *No.* I'm as good a judge of a cat's character, I am, as hanyone. I knowed that there cat soon's I seed 'im. I says, 'There's a hanimal as will curl up anywheres you like ter put 'im an' so long's 'e's got 'is cushion an' 'is saucer o' milk regular, 'e won't 'anker after nuffin' else. 'E won't go no long torchurous road journeys tryin' to find old 'omes. Not 'e. 'E'll rub 'isself against hanyone wot'll say 'Puss, puss.' 'Sides which it's agin' my feelings as a 'umane man to put to death a young an' 'ealthy hanimal."

William stared at him.

"Now, the second one, you brought, well, 'e was ripe fer death, all right, an' it's a pleasure an' kindness to do it in those circs. 'Sides which," Mr. Gorton went on as another argument occurred to him, "wot proof 'ave you that this 'ere hanimal of Miss Cliff's is the same hanimal wot you brought to me Saturday? They're both black cats—no marks on 'em. Well, there must be 'undreds of black cats same as that—thahsands—*millions*—just think of 'em—all hover the world. Well, jus' you prove that these two hanimals is identical."

William, having for once in his life met his match in eloquence, moved away despondently.

"All right," he said, "I only asked." He went to the parrot who was still there, and who greeted him with an ironical laugh and a cry of: "My *word*—what a nut! Oh, my *word!*"

William's spirits rose.

"How much is the parrot?" he said.

"Five pounds," said Mr. Gorton.

William's spirits sank again.

"Snakes one and six—and—and, see here, I'll *give* you a baby tortoise jus' to stop you worrying about that hanimal."

William walked home proudly carrying his baby tortoise in both hands.

Miss Amelia Blake was in the drawing-room. She was speaking tearfully to his mother. "And I leave his saucer of milk out every night and I call him every night, my poor Luky. I can hardly sleep with thinking of my darling, perhaps hungry and needing me . . . William, if you see any traces of my Luky you'll let me know, won't you?"

And William, oppressed by the weight of his guilty secret, muttered something inaudible and went to watch the effect of his new pet upon Jumble.

That night the plaintive cry arose again to his room.

"Luky, Luky, Luky, Luky, Luk-ee-ee-*ee!* Luky, Luky. Where *are* you, darling? Luky, Luky, Luky, Luky, Lukee-ee-ee-ee."

* * *

William's conscience, though absolved of the crime of murder, felt heavy as Miss Amelia Blake called her lost pet mournfully night after night.

Now William's conscience was a curious organ. It needed a great deal to rouse it. When roused it demanded immediate action. He took one of his white rats round to Miss Amelia Blake, and Miss Amelia Blake screamed and got on to the table. He even rose to supreme heights of self-denial, and offered her his baby tortoise, but she refused it.

"No, William dear, it's very kind of you, but what I need is something I can stroke—and I don't want anything but my Luky—and I—I don't like its expression—it looks as if it might bite. I *couldn't* stroke that!"

Greatly relieved, William took it back.

That afternoon, perched on the garden fence, his elbows on his knees, his chin in his hands, he watched the antics of Jumble round the baby tortoise. Though William had had the tortoise for three days now, Jumble still barked at it with unabated fury, and William watched the two with unabated interest. But William's thoughts were still occupied with the Twinkie-Luky problem. The ethics of the case were difficult. It belonged to Miss Blake, but Miss Cliff had paid for it. Then suddenly the solution occurred to him—a week each. They should have it a week each—that would be quite easy to manage. His heart lightened. He jumped down, put his tortoise into his pocket, called "Hi, Jumble!" took a stick, jumped (almost) over the bed in the middle of the lawn, and went whistling down the road followed by Jumble.

The covered basket was very old and very shabby, and it did not need much persuasion on William's part to induce Mrs. Brown to give it to him.

"Jus' to keep my things in an' carry 'em about in, mother," he said plaintively, "so as I won't be so untidy. I shan't be half as untidy if I have a basket like that to keep my things in an' carry 'em about in."

"All right, dear," said Mrs. Brown, much pleased.

She was eternally optimistic about William.

William spent an entire Saturday morning stalking Luky in the neighbourhood of Miss Cliff's garden (Miss Cliff went into the town to do her shopping on Saturday mornings). Finally he caught him, put him in the basket, and secretly deposited Luky in Miss Amelia Blake's garden. Miss Blake was overjoyed.

"He's come back, Mrs. Brown! Mrs. Brown, he's come back. William, he's come back—Luky's come back."

Miss Cliff was distraught.

"Little boy, you haven't seen my Twinkie anywhere, have you? My darling Twinkie, he's gone. Twinkie! Twinkie! Twinkie! Twinkie! Twinkie-ee-*ee!*"

The next four Saturdays he successfully changed Twinkie-Luky's place of abode. On arrival at Miss Cliff's Twinkie made immediately for his favourite cushion and went to sleep. On arrival at Miss Amelia Blake's Luky did the same. The owners became almost accustomed to the week's mysterious absence.

"He's gone away again, Mrs. Brown," Miss Blake would call over the fence. "I only hope he'll come back as he did last time. You haven't seen him, have you? Luky, Luky, Luky, Luky, Lukee-ee-ee-ee-*ee!*"

Then William became bored. At first the glorious consciousness of duty done and the salving of his sense of guilt had upheld him, but he began to feel that this could not go on for ever. When all is said and done, Saturday is Saturday—a golden holiday in a drab procession of schooldays. William began to think that if he had to spend every Saturday of his life stalking Twinkie-Luky and conveying him secretly from one end of the village to the other, he might just as well not have been born——

*   *   *

He had put Twinky-Luky in the basket and was setting off with it down the road. It was very hot and Twinkie-Luky was very heavy and William was very cross. He had just come to the conclusion that some other solution must be found to the Twinkie-Luky problem when he heard the sound of the 'bus that made its slow and noisy progress from the neighbouring country town to the village in which William lived.

A ride in the 'bus would save him a long, hot walk with the heavy basket, and by some miraculous chance he had the requisite penny in his pocket. And anyhow, he was sick of the whole thing. He hailed the bus by swinging the basket round and putting out his tongue at the driver. The driver put his out in return, and the 'bus stopped. William, holding the basket, entered. The 'bus was very full, but there was one empty seat. William had taken this seat before he realised with horror that on one side of him sat Miss Amelia Blake and on the other Miss Cliff.

The 'bus had started again, and it was too late to get out. He went rather pale, pretended not to see them, stared in front of him with a set, stern expression on his face, and clasped the basket containing Twinkie-Luky tightly to his bosom. Miss Amelia Blake and Miss Cliff did not "know" each other. But they both knew William.

"Good morning, little boy," said Miss Cliff.

"Mornin'," muttered William, still staring straight in front of him.

"Good morning, William," said Miss Blake.

"Mornin'," muttered William.

"Have you been doing some shopping for your mother?" said Miss Blake brightly.

"Uumph!" said William, his eyes still fixed desperately on the opposite window, the basket still clutched tightly to his breast.

"You must call and see my pussy again soon, little boy," said Miss Cliff.

A shadow passed over Miss Amelia Blake's face.

"You haven't seen Luky, have you, William? He's been away all this week."

William felt a spasmodic movement in the basket at the sound of the name. He moistened his lips and shook his head.

Miss Amelia Blake was looking with interest at his basket. It happened that she wanted a new shopping basket, and had called at the basket-shop about one that morning.

"May I look at your basket, William?" she said kindly. "I like these covered baskets for shopping. The things can't tumble out. On the other hand, of course, you can't get so many things in. Are the fastenings firm?"

Her hand was outstretched innocently towards the fastenings. A cold perspiration broke out over William. He put his hands desperately over his fastenings.

"LUKY!" CRIED MISS BLAKE.
"TWINKIE!" EXCLAIMED MISS CLIFF.
"HE'S MINE!"
"HE ISN'T!"

"I wun't—I wun't touch 'em," he said hoarsely.
"It's—it's a bit full. I wun't like all the things to come
tumblin' out here."

Miss Amelia Blake smiled agreement and Miss Cliff
beamed on him from the other side. William was wishing
that the earth would open and swallow up Miss Amelia
Blake and Miss Cliff and Twinkie-Luky and himself.

At last the 'bus stopped at the cross-road and they all
got out. William's relief was indescribable. *That* was

A BLACK HEAD AROSE FROM THE BASKET AND PURRED.

over. And it was the last time *he'd* ever change their ole cats for 'em. He turned to go down the road, but Miss Amelia Blake put her hand on his arm.

"I'll hold it very carefully, William," she pleaded. "I won't let anything tumble out, but I *do* want to see if the fastenings of these baskets are secure."

Miss Cliff stood by smiling with interested curiosity. William mutely abandoned himself to Fate. Miss Amelia Blake opened one fastening, the flap turned back, and a black-whiskered head arose and looked around with a purr.

"Luky!"

"Twinkie!"

"He's mine."

"I bought him at Mr. Gorton's."

"How *can* you say he's yours?"

"He's mine," cried Miss Cliff.

"He isn't," retorted Miss Blake.

"He knows me—*Twinkie!*"

"*Luky!*"

Both made a grab at Twinkie-Luky, but Twinkie-Luky escaped both and flew like a dart down the road in the direction of Mr. Gorton's. Like all real gentlemen, Twinkie-Luky preferred death to a scene. William was no coward, but even a braver man than William would have fled. William's fleeing figure was already half-way down the road in which his home lay.

At the cross-roads Miss Amelia Blake and Miss Cliff clung to each other hysterically and sent forth shrill, discordant cries after the fleeing Twinkie-Luky.

"Twinkie, Twinkie, Twinkie, Twinkie, Twink-ee-ee-ee-ee-*ee!*"

"Luky, Luky, Luky, Luky, Lukee-ee-ee-ee-*ee!*"

And William ran as if all the cats in the world were at his heels.

Chapter 10

William the Showman

William and his friends, known to themselves as the Outlaws, were in their usual state of insolvency. All entreaties had failed to melt the heart of Mr. Beezum, the keeper of the general store in the village, who sold marbles, along with such goods as hams and shoes and vegetables.

William and his friends wanted marbles—simply a few dozen of ordinary glass marbles which could be bought for a few pence. But Mr. Beezum refused to overlook the small matter of the few pence. He refused to give the Outlaws credit.

"My terms to you, young gents, is cash down, an' well you know it," he said firmly.

"If you," said William generously, "let us have the marbles now we'll give you a halfpenny extra Saturday."

"You said that once before, young gent, if I remember right," said Mr. Beezum, adjusting his capacious apron and turning up his shirt-sleeves preparatory to sweeping out his shop.

William was indignant at the suggestion.

"Well," he said, "*well*—you talk 's if that was *my* fault—'s if I knew my people was going to decide sudden not to give me any money that week *simply* because one of their cucumber frames got broke by my ball. An' I brought back the things wot you'd let me have. I brought the trumpet back *an'* the rock——"

"Yes—the trumpet all broke an' the rock all bit," said Mr. Beezum. "No—cash down is my terms, an' I sticks to 'em—if *you* please, young gents."

He began his sweeping operations with great energy, and the Outlaws found themselves precipitated into the street by the end of his long broom.

"Mean," commented William, rising again to the perpendicular. "Jus' *mean!* I've a good mind not to buy 'em there at all."

"He's the only shop that sells 'em," remarked Ginger.

"An' we've got no money to buy 'em anywhere, anyway," said Henry.

"S'pose we couldn't wait for 'em till Saturday?" suggested Douglas tentatively.

He was promptly crushed by the Outlaws.

"*Wait!*" said Ginger. "*Wait!* Wot's the use of waitin'? We may be doing something else on Saturday. We mayn't *want* to play with marbles—all that long time off."

"'F only you'd *save* your money," said William severely, "'stead of spendin' it the day you get it we shun't be like this—no marbles, an' swep' out of his shop an' nothin to play at."

This was felt to be unfair.

"Well, I like *that*—I *like* that," said Ginger. "And wot about *you*—wot about *you?*"

"Well, if I was the only one, you could have lent me money an' we could get marbles with it—if *you'd* not spent all your money we could be buyin' marbles now 'stead of standin' swep' out of his shop."

Ginger thought over this, aware that there was usually some fallacy in William's arguments if only one could lay one's hand on it.

Henry turned away.

"Oh, come along," he said impatiently. "It's no good staring in at his ole butter an' cheese. Let's think of something else to do."

"Anyway, it's nasty cheese," said Douglas comfortingly. "My mother said it was—so p'raps it's a good thing we've been saved buyin' his marbles."

"Something else to do?" said William. "We want to play marbles, don't we? Wot's the good of thinkin' of other things when we want to play marbles?"

"'S all very well to talk like that," said Ginger with sudden inspiration, "an' we might jus' as well say that 'f you'd not spent your money you could have lent us some, an' that's just as much sense as you saying if *we*——"

"Oh, do shut up talkin' stuff no one can understand," said William, "let's *get* some money."

"How?" said Ginger, who was nettled. "All right. Get some, an' we'll watch you. You goin' to *steal* some or *make* some. 'F you're clever enough to steal some *or* make some I'll be very glad to join with it."

"Yes, well, if I stole some or made some you just *wouldn't* join with it," said William crushingly.

"Let's sell something," said Henry.

"We've got nothing anyone'd buy," said Ginger.

"Let's sell Jumble."

"Jumble's *mine*. You can jus' sell your own dogs," said William, sternly.

"We've not got any."

"Well, then, sell 'em."

"That's sense, isn't it?" said Ginger. "Jus' kindly tell us how to sell dogs we've not got—— Jus'——"

But William was suddenly tired of this type of verbal warfare.

"Let's do something—let's have a show."

"Wot of?" said Ginger without enthusiasm. "We've got nothing to show, an' who'll pay us money to look at nothing. Jus' tell us that."

"We'll get something to show—I *know*," he said suddenly, "a c'lection of insecks. Anyone'd pay to see an exhibition of a c'lection of insecks, wun't they? I don't s'pose there are many c'lections of insecks, anyway. It'd be *interestin'*. Everyone's interested in *insecks*."

For a minute the Outlaws wavered.

"Who'd c'lect 'em?" said Henry, dubiously.

"I would," said William with an air of stern purpose.

*   *   *

The Collection of Insects was almost complete. The show was to be held that afternoon.

The audience had been ordered to attend and bring their halfpennies. The audience had agreed, but had reserved to itself the right not to contribute the halfpennies if the exhibition was not considered worth it.

"Well," was William's bitter comment on hearing this, "I shouldn't have thought there was so many *mean* people in the world."

He had taken a great deal of trouble with his collection. He had that very morning been driven out of Miss Euphemia Barney's garden by Miss Euphemia herself, though he had only entered in pursuit of a yellow butterfly that he felt was indispensable to the collection.

Miss Euphemia Barney was the local poetess and the leader of the intellectual life of the village. Miss Euphemia Barney was the President of the Society for the Encouragement of Higher Thought. The members of the society discussed Higher Thought in all its branches once every fortnight. At the end of the discussion Miss Euphemia Barney would read her poems.

Euphemia Barney's poems had never been published. Miss Euphemia said that in these days of worldliness and money-worship she would set an example of unworldliness and scorn for money. "I think it best," she would say, "that I should not publish."

As a matter of fact she had the authority of several publishers for the statement. She disliked William more than anyone else she had ever known—and she said that she knew just what sort of a woman Miss Fairlow was as soon as she heard that Miss Fairlow had "taken to" William.

Miss Fairlow had only recently come to live at the village. Miss Fairlow was a real, live, worldly, money-worshipping author who published a book every year and made a lot of money out of it. When she came to live in the village Miss Euphemia Barney was prepared to patronise her in spite of this fact, and even asked her to join the Society for the Encouragement of Higher Thought.

But, to the surprise of Miss Euphemia, Miss Fairlow refused.

Miss Euphemia pitied her as she would have pitied anyone who had refused the golden chance of belonging to the Society for the Encouragement of Higher Thought under her—Miss Euphemia Barney's—presidency, but, as she said to the Society, "her influence would not have tended to the unworldliness and purity that distinguishes us from so many other societies and bodies—it is all for the best."

To her most intimate friends she said that Miss Fairlow had refused the offer of membership in order to mask her complete ignorance of Higher Thought.

"Ignorant, my dear," she said. "Ignorant—like all these popular writers."

So the Society for the Encouragement of Higher Thought pursued its pure and unworldly path, and Miss Fairlow only laughed at it from a distance.

*   *   *

Chased ignominiously from Miss Euphemia's garden, William went along to Miss Fairlow's. He could see her over the hedge mowing the lawn.

"Hello," he said.

"Hello, William," she replied.

"Got any insects there?" said William.

"Heaps. Come in and see."

William came in with a business-like air—his large cardboard box under his arm—and began to hunt among her garden plants.

"Would you call a tortoise an insect?" he said suddenly.

"If I wanted to," she replied.

"Well, I'm going to," said William firmly. "And I'm going to call a white rat an insect."

"I don't see why you shouldn't—it might belong to a special branch of the insect world, a very special branch. You ought to give it a very special name."

The idea appealed to William.

"All right. What name?"

Miss Fairlow rested against the handle of her lawn mower in an attitude of profound meditation.

"We must consider that—something nice and long."

"Omshafu," said William suddenly, after a moment's thought. "It just came," he went on modestly, "just came into my head."

"It's a beautiful word," said Miss Fairlow. "I don't

think you could have a better one—an insect of the Omshafu branch.''

"I think I'll call its name Omshafu, too," said William, picking a furry caterpillar off a leaf.

"Yes," said Miss Fairlow, "it seems a pity not to use a word like that as much as you can now you've thought of it.''

William put a ladybird in on top of the caterpillar.

"It's going to be jolly fine," he said optimistically.

"What?" said Miss Fairlow.

"Oh, jus' a c'lection of insects I'm doing," said William.

Later in the morning, William brought Omshafu over to visit Miss Fairlow. It escaped, and Miss Fairlow pursued it up her front stairs and down her back ones, and finally captured it. Omshafu rewarded her by biting her finger. William was apologetic.

"I daresay it just didn't like the look of me," said Miss Fairlow sadly.

"Oh, no," William hastened to reassure her; "it's bit heaps of people this year—it bites people it likes. I don't say why it *shun't* be an insect, anyway, do you?''

*   *   *

William's Collection of Insects was ready for the afternoon's show. The exhibits were arranged in small cardboard boxes, covered mostly with paper, and these were all packed into a large cardboard box.

The only difficulty was that he could not think where to conceal it from curious or disapproving eyes till after lunch. The garden, he felt, was not safe—cats might upset it, and once upset in the garden the insects would be able to return to their native haunts too quickly. His mother would not allow him to keep them indoors. She would find them and expel them wherever he put them.

Unless—William had a brilliant idea—he hid them under the drawing-room sofa. The drawing-room sofa had a cretonne cover with a frill that reached to the floor, and he had used this place before as a temporary receptacle for secret treasures. No one would look under it, or think of his putting anything there. He put the tortoise into a box with a lid, and tied Omshafu up firmly with string in his box, and put them in the large cardboard box with the insects. Then he put the large cardboard box under the sofa and went into lunch with a mind freed from anxiety.

The exhibition was not to begin till three, so William wandered out to find Jumble. He found him in the ditch, threw sticks for him, brushed him severely with an old boot brush that he kept in the outhouse for the rare occasions of Jumble's toilet, and finally tied round his neck the old, raggy and almost colourless pink ribbon that was his gala attire. Then he came to the drawing-room for the exhibits. There he received his first shock.

On the drawing-room sofa sat Miss Euphemia Barney, wearing her very highest thought expression. She surveyed William from head to foot silently with a look of slight disgust, then turned away her head with a shudder. William sought his mother.

"Wot's she *doin*' in our house?" he demanded sternly.

"I've lent the drawing-room for a meeting of the Higher Thought, darling," said Mrs. Brown reverently, "because she has the painters in her own drawing-room. You mustn't interrupt."

Mrs. Brown was not a Higher Thinker, but she cherished a deep respect for them.

"But——" began William indignantly, then stopped. He thought, upon deliberation, that it was better not to betray his hiding-place.

He went back to the drawing-room determined to

walk boldly up to the sofa and drag out the exhibits from under the very skirts of Miss Euphemia Barney. But two more Higher Thinkers were now established upon the sofa, one on each side of the President, and Higher Thinkers were pouring into the room. William's courage failed him. He sat down upon a chair by the door scowling, his eyes fixed upon Miss Euphemia's skirts.

The members looked at him with lofty disapproval. The gathering was complete. The meeting was about to begin. Miss Euphemia Barney was to speak on the Commoner Complexes. But first she turned upon William, who sat with his eyes fixed forlornly on the hem of her skirts, a devastating glare.

"Do you want anything, little boy?" she said.

Before William had time to tell her what he wanted the maid threw open the door and announced Miss Fairlow. The Higher Thinkers gasped. Miss Fairlow looked round as Daniel must have looked round at his lions.

"I came——" she said. "Oh, dear!"

Miss Euphemia waved her to a seat. It occurred to her that here was a heaven-sent opportunity of impressing Miss Fairlow with a real respect for Higher Thought. Miss Fairlow must learn how much higher they were in thought than she could ever be. It would be a great triumph to enlist Miss Fairlow as a humble member and searcher after truth under her—Miss Euphemia's—leadership.

"You came to see Mrs. Brown, of course," she said kindly, "and the maid showed you in here thinking you were—ahem—one of us. Mrs. Brown has kindly lent us her drawing-room for a meeting. Pray don't apologise—perhaps you would like to listen to us for a short time. We were about to discuss the Commoner Complexes. I will begin by reading a little poem. I spent most of this

morning putting the final touches to it," she ended
proudly.

"I spent most of this morning on the pursuit of
Omshafu," said Miss Fairlow gravely.

There was a moment's tense silence. Omshafu? The
Higher Thinkers sent glances of desperate appeal to
their president. Would she allow them to be humiliated
by this upstart?

"Ah, Omshafu!" said Miss Euphemia slowly. "Of
couse it—it *is* very interesting."

The Higher Thinkers gave a sigh of relief.

"I could hardly tear myself away this morning,"
replied Miss Fairlow pleasantly. "It was so engrossing."
Engrossing! Some sort of Eastern philosophy, of course.
Again desperate glances were turned upon the embodi-
ment of Higher Thought. Again she rose to the
occasion.

"I felt just the same about it when I—er—when I,"
she risked the expression, "took it up."

She felt that this implied that she had known about
Omshafu long before Miss Fairlow, and this conveyed a
delicate snub.

Miss Fairlow's glance rested momentarily on her
bandaged finger.

"It goes very deep," she murmured.

Miss Barney was gaining confidence.

"There I agree with you," she said firmly. "I think its
appeal is entirely superficial."

William had brightened into attention at the first
mention of Omshafu, but finding the conversation
beyond him, had relapsed into a gloomy stare. Now his
stare became suddenly fixed; his mouth opened with
horror.

The exhibits were escaping from beneath the hem of
Miss Euphemia's gown. A cockroach was making a slow

and stately progress into the middle of the room, several ants were laboriously climbing up Miss Euphemia's dress. So far no one else had noticed. William gazed in frozen horror.

"I hear that Omshafu has bitten most people this year," said Miss Fairlow demurely.

Miss Euphemia pursed her lips disapprovingly. She was growing reckless with success. "I think there's something dangerous in it," she said.

"You mean its teeth?" said Miss Fairlow brightly.

There was a moment's tense silence. A horrible suspicion occurred to Miss Euphemia that she was being trifled with. The Higher Thinkers looked helplessly first at her and then at Miss Fairlow. Then Miss Euphemia rose from the sofa with a piercing scream.

"Something's stung me! It's bees—bees coming from under the sofa!"

Simultaneously the Treasurer jumped upon a small occasional table.

"Black beetles!" she screamed. "Help!"

Above the babel rose Miss Fairlow's clear voice.

"And there's Omshafu himself. I can see his dear little pink nose peeping out."

Babel ceased for one second while the Society for the Encouragement of Higher Thought looked at Omshafu. Then it arose with redoubled violence.

*   *   *

William departed with his exhibits. He had recaptured most of them. Omshafu had been taken from the ample silk sash of the Treasurer in a fold of which he had taken refuge. William had left his mother and Miss Fairlow pouring water on the hysterical Treasurer.

William was late as it was. Behind him trotted Jumble,

"THERE'S OMSHAFU HIMSELF," SAID MISS FAIRLOW IN HER
CLEAR VOICE. "I CAN SEE HIS DEAR LITTLE PINK NOSE PEEPING
OUT."

the chewed-up remains of his gala attire hanging from
his mouth.

"William."

Miss Fairlow was just behind, carrying a cardboard
box.

MISS EUPHEMIA JUMPED UP WITH A PIERCING SCREAM.
"SOMETHING STUNG ME!" SHE CRIED. "IT'S BEES COMING FROM
UNDER THE SOFA!"

"Oh, William," she said, "I was really bringing this to
you when they showed me into the wrong room and I
couldn't resist having a game with them. I found it this
morning after you'd gone—in an old drawer I was
tidying, and I thought you might like it."

William opened it. It was a case of butterflies—butterflies of every kind, all neatly labelled.

"I think it used to belong to my brother," said Miss Fairlow carelessly. "Would you like it?"

"Oh, *crumbs!*" gasped William. "*Thanks.*"

"And I've had the loveliest time this afternoon that I've had for ages," said Miss Fairlow dreamily. "Thank you so much."

William hastened to the old barn in which the Exhibition was to be held. Ginger, Douglas and Henry and the audience were already there.

"Well, you're early, aren't you?" said Douglas sarcastically.

"*D'you think*," said William sternly, "that anyone wot has had all the hard work I've had getting together this c'lection could be here *earlier?*"

The half-dozen little boys who formed the audience grasped their halfpennies firmly and looked at William suspiciously.

"They won't give up their halfpennies," said Henry in deep disgust.

"No," said the audience, "not till we've seen if it's *worth* a halfpenny."

William assumed his best showman air.

"This, ladies and gentlemen," he began, ignoring the fact that his audience consisted entirely of males, "is the only tortoise like this in the world."

"Seen a tortoise." "Got a tortoise at home," said his audience unimpressed.

"*Perhaps*," said William crushingly. "But have you ever seen a tortoise with white stripes like wot this one has?"

"No, but I could if I got an ole tin of paint and striped our one."

William passed on to the next box.

He took out Omshafu.

"*This*," he said, "is the only rat inseck of the speeshees of Omshafu——"

"If you think," said the audience, "that we're goin' to pay a halfpenny to see that ole rat wot we've seen hundreds of times before, and wot's bit us, too—well, we're *not*."

Despair began to settle down upon Ginger's face.

William passed on to the third box.

"Here, ladies and gentlemen," he said impressively, "is thirty sep'rate *an'* distinct speeshees of insecks. I only ask you to look at them. I——"

"They're jus' the same sort of insecks as crawl about our garden at home," said the audience coldly.

"But have you ever seen 'em c'lected *together* before?" said William earnestly. "Have you ever seen 'em *c'lected?* Think of the trouble an' time wot I took c'lecting 'em. Why, the time alone I took's worth more'n a halfpenny. I should *think* that's worth a halfpenny. I should think it's worth more'n a halfpenny. I should think——"

"Well, we wun't," said the audience. "We'd as soon see 'em crawling about a garden for nothin' as crawlin' about a box for a halfpenny. So there."

Ginger, Douglas and Henry looked at William gloomily.

"They aren't *worth* getting a c'lection for," said Ginger.

"They deserve to have their halfpennies *took* off em!" said Douglas.

But William slowly and majestically brought out his fourth box and opened it, revealing rows of gorgeous butterflies, then closed it quickly.

The audience gasped.

"When you've given in your halfpennies," said

William firmly, "then you can see this wonderfu' an' unique c'election of twenty sep'rate *an*' distinct speeshees of butterflies all c'lected together."

Eagerly the halfpennies were given to William. He handed them to Douglas, triumphantly. "Go an' buy the marbles, quick," he said in a hoarse whisper, "'case they want 'em back."

Then he turned to his audience, smoothed back his hair, and reassumed his showman manner.

* * *

In Mrs. Brown's drawing-room the members of the Society for the Encouragement of Higher Thought were recovering from various stages of hysterics.

"We shall have to dissolve the society," said Miss Euphemia Barney. "She'll tell everyone. It's a wicked name for a rat, anyway—almost blasphemous—I'm sure it comes in the Bible. How was one to know? But people will never forget it."

"We might form ourselves again a little later under a different name," suggested the Secretary.

"People will always remember," said Miss Euphemia. "They're so uncharitable. It's a most unfortunate occurrence. And," setting her lips grimly, "as is the case with most of the unfortunate occurrences in this village, the direct cause is that terrible boy, William Brown."

At that moment the direct cause of most of the unfortunate occurrences in the village, with his friends around him, his precious box of butterflies by his side, and happiness in his heart, was just beginning the hard-won, long-deferred game of marbles.

Chapter 11

William's Extra Day

"What's Leap Year?" asked William.

"It's a year that leaps," said his elder brother, Robert.

"It's Leap Year this year," said William.

"Who told you?" inquired Robert sarcastically.

"Well, I don't see much leapin' about this year so far," said William, trying to rise to equal heights of sarcasm.

"Oh, go and play Leap Frog," said Robert scathingly.

"I don't believe you *know*," said William. "I don't for a minute b'lieve you know why it's called Leap Year. You don't care, either. S'long as you can sit talkin' to Miss Flower, you don't care about anything else. You've not even got any curiosity 'bout Leap Year nor anything else. I dunno what you find to talk to her about. I bet she doesn't know why it's Leap Year no more than you do. You don't talk 'bout anything sensible—you an' Miss Flower. You——"

Robert's youthful countenance had flushed a dull red. Miss Flower was the latest of Robert's seemingly endless and quickly changing succession of grand passions.

"You don't even talk most of the time," went on William scornfully, "'cause I've watched you. You sit lookin'—jus' *lookin'*—at each other like wot you used to with Miss Crane an' Miss Blake an' Miss—what was she called? An' it does look soft, let me *tell* you, to anyone watchin' through the window."

Robert rose with murder in his eye.

"Shut *up* and get *out!*" he roared.

William shut up and got out. He sighed as he wandered into the garden. It was like Robert to get into a temper just because somebody asked him quite politely what Leap Year was.

Ethel, William's grown-up sister, was in the drawing-room.

"Ethel," said William, "why's it called Leap Year?"

"Because of February 29th," said Ethel.

"Well," said William, with an air of patience tried beyond endurance, "if you think that's any answer to anyone askin' you why's it Leap Year—if you think that's an answer that *means* anythin' to any ornery person . . ."

"You see, everything leaps on February 29th," said his sister callously; "you wait and see."

William looked at her in silent scorn for a few moments, then gave vent to his feelings.

"Anyone'd think that anyone's old as you an' Robert would know a simple thing like that. Jus' think of you *an'* Robert *an'* Miss Flower not knowing why it's called Leap Year."

"How do you know Miss Flower doesn't know?"

"Well, wun't she have told Robert if she knew? She must have told Robert everythin' she knows by this time, talkin' to him an' talkin' to him like she does. F' that matter I don't s'pose Mr. Brooke knows. He'd have told you 'f he did. He's always——"

Ethel groaned.

"Will you stop talking and go away if I give you a chocolate?" she said.

William forgot his grievance.

"Three," he stipulated in a quick business-like voice. "Gimme three 'n I'll go *right* away."

She gave him three so readily that he regretted not having asked for six.

He put two in his mouth, pocketed the third, and went into the morning-room.

His father was there reading a newspaper.

"Father," said William, "why's it called Leap Year?"

"How many times am I to tell you," said his father, "to shut the door when you come into a room? There's an icy blast piercing down my neck now. Do you want to murder me?"

"No, father," said William kindly. He shut the door. "Father, why's it called Leap Year?"

"Ask your mother," said his father, without looking up from his paper.

"She mightn't know."

"Well, ask someone else then. Ask anyone in heaven or earth. BUT DON'T ASK ME ANYTHING! And shut the door when you go out."

William, though as a rule slow to take a hint, went out of the room and shut the door.

"*He* doesn't know," he remarked to the hat-rack in the hall.

He found his mother in the dining-room. She was engaged in her usual occupation of darning socks.

"Mother," said William, "why's it called Leap Year?"

"I simply can't *think*, William," said Mrs. Brown feelingly, "how do you get such *dreadful* holes in your heels?"

"It's that hard road on the way to school, I 'spect," said William. "I've gotter walk to school. I 'spect that's it. I 'spect 'f I didn't go to school an' kept to the fields an' woods I wun't gettem like wot I do. But you an'

father keep sayin' I've gotter
go to school. I wun't mind not
goin'—jus' to save you trouble.
I wun't mind growin' up
ign'rant like wot you say I
would if I didn't go to school—
jus' to save you trouble—I——"

Mrs. Brown hastily interrupted him.

"What did you want to know,
William?"

William returned to his
quest.

"Why's it called Leap Year?"

"Well," said Mrs. Brown, "it's because of February
29th. It's an extra day."

William thought over this for some time in silence.

"D'you mean," he said at last, "that it's an extra day
that doesn't count in the ornery year?"

"Yes, that's it," said Mrs. Brown vaguely. "William
dear, I wish you wouldn't always stand *just* in my light."

*   *   *

It was February 29th. William was unusually silent
during breakfast. In the relief caused by his silence his
air of excitement was unnoticed.

After breakfast, William went upstairs. He took two
small paper parcels from a drawer and put them into his
overcoat pocket. One contained several small cakes
surreptitiously abstracted from the larder, the other
contained William's "disguise." William's "disguise"
was a false beard which had formed part of Robert's
hired costume for the Christmas theatricals. Robert
never knew what had happened to the beard. He had

been charged for it as "missing" by the theatrical costumier.

William had felt that a "disguise" was a necessity to him. All the heroes of the romances he read found it necessary in the crises of their adventurous lives to assume disguises. William felt that you never knew when a crisis was coming, and that any potential hero of adventure—such as he knew himself to be—should never allow himself to be without a "disguise." So far he had not had need to assume it. But he had hopes for to-day. It was an extra day. Surely you could do just what you liked on an extra day. To-day was to be a day of adventure.

He went downstairs and put on his cap in the hall.

"You'll be rather early for school," said Mrs. Brown.

William's unsmiling countenance assumed a look of virtue.

"I don't mind bein' early for school," he said.

Slowly and decorously he went down the drive and disappeared from sight.

Mrs. Brown went back to the dining-room where her husband was still reading the paper.

"William's so good today," she said.

Her husband groaned.

"Eight-thirty in the morn-ing," he said, "and she says he's good to-day! My dear, he's not had time to look round yet!"

William walked down the road with a look of set pur-pose on his face. Near the school he met Bertram Roke. Bertram Roke was the good boy of the school.

"You're not goin' to school to-day, are you?" said William.

"Course," said Bertram virtuously. "Aren't you?"

"Me?" said William. "Don't you know what day it is? Don't you know it's an extra day wot doesn't count in the ornery year. Catch *me* goin' to school on an extra day what doesn't count in the ornery year."

"What are you goin' to do, then?" said Bertram, taken aback.

"I'm goin' to have adventures."

"You'll—you'll miss geography," said Bertram.

"Geography!" said the hero of adventures scornfully.

Leaving Bertram gaping over the school wall, his Latin grammar under one arm and his geography book under the other, William walked up the hill and into the wood in search of adventures.

*   *   *

It was most certainly a gipsy encampment. There was a pot boiling on a camp fire and a crowd of ragged children playing around. Three caravans stood on the broad cart track that led through the wood.

William watched the children wistfully from a distance. More than anything on earth at that moment William longed to be a gipsy. He approached the children. All of them fled behind the caravans except one—a very dirty boy in a ragged green jersey and ragged knickers and bare legs. He squared his fists and knocked William down. William jumped up and knocked the boy down. The boy knocked William down again, but overbalanced with the effort. They sat on the ground and looked at each other.

"Wot's yer nyme?" said the boy.

"William. Wot's yours?"

"Helbert. Wot yer doin' 'ere?"

"Lookin' for adventures," said William. "It's an extra day, you know. I want to-day to be quite diff'rent from an ornery day. I want some adventures; I'd like to be a gipsy, too," he ended wistfully.

Helbert merely stared at him.

"Would they take me?" went on William, nodding his head in the direction of the caravans. "I'd soon learn to be a gipsy. I'd do all they tell me. I've always wanted to be a gipsy—next to a Red Indian and a pirate, and there don't seem to be any Red Indians or pirates in this country."

Helbert once more merely stared at him. William's hopes sank.

"I've not got any gipsy clothes," he said, "but p'raps they'd give me some."

Enviously William looked at Helbert's ragged jersey and knickers and bare feet. Enviously Helbert looked at William's suit. Suddenly Helbert's heavy face lightened. He pointed to William's suit.

"Swop," he said, succinctly.

"Don't you really mind?" said William, humbly and gratefully.

The exchange was effected behind a bush. William carefully transferred his packet of provisions and his disguise from his pocket to the pocket of Helbert's ragged knickers. Then, while Helbert was still donning waistcoat and coat, William swaggered into the open space round the fire. His heart was full to bursting. He was a gipsy of the gipsies.

"'Ello," he called, in swaggering friendly greeting to the gipsy children. But his friendliness was not returned.

"'E's stole Helbert's clothes."

"You wait till my Dad ketches yer. 'E'll wallop year."

"Ma! 'E's got our Helbert's jersey on."

A woman appeared suddenly at the door of the

caravan. She was larger and dirtier and fiercer-looking than anyone William had ever seen before. She advanced upon William, and William, forgetting his dignity as a hero of adventures, fled through the wood in terror, till he could flee no more.

Then he stopped, and discovering that the fat woman was not pursuing him, sat down and leant against a tree to rest. He took out his crumpled packet of provisions, ate one cake and put the rest back again into his pocket. He felt that his extra day had opened propitiously. He was a gipsy. William never felt happier than when he had completely shed his own identity.

He did not regret leaving the members of the gipsy encampment. He had not really liked the look of any of them. There had been something unfriendly even about Helbert. He preferred to be a gipsy on his own. He ran and leapt. He turned cart wheels. He climbed trees. He was riotously happy. He was a gipsy.

Suddenly he saw a little old man stretched out at full length beneath a tree. The little old man was watching something in the grass through a magnifying glass. On one side of him lay a notebook, on the other a large japanned tin case. William, full of curiosity, crept cautiously towards him through the grass on the other side of the tree. He peered round the tree-trunk, and the little old man, looking up suddenly, found William's face within a few inches of his own.

"Sh!" said the little old man. "A rare specimen! Ah! Gone! My movement, I am afraid. Never mind. I had it under observation for quite fifteen minutes. And I have a specimen of it."

He began to write in his notebook. Then he looked up again at William.

"Who are you, boy?" he said suddenly.

"I'm a gipsy," said William proudly.

"What's your name?"

"Helbert," said William without hesitation.

"Well, Albert," said the little old gentleman, "would you like to earn sixpence by carrying this case to my house? It's just at the end of the wood."

Without a word William took the case and set off beside the little old gentleman. The little old gentleman carried the notebook, and William carried the japanned tin case.

"An interesting life, a gipsy's, I should think," said the old gentleman.

Memories of stories he had read about gipsies returned to William.

"I wasn't born a gipsy," he said. 'I was stole by the gipsies when I was a baby."

The little old gentleman turned to peer at William over his spectacles.

"Really?" he said. "That's interesting—most interesting. What are your earliest recollections previous to being stolen?"

William was thoroughly enjoying himself. He was William no longer. He was not even Helbert. He was Evelyn de Vere, the hero of "Stolen by Gipsies," which he had read a few months ago.

"Oh, I remember a kinder palace an' a garden with stachues an' peacocks an'—er—waterfalls an'—er—flowers and things, an' a black man what came in the night an' took me off, an' I've gotter birthmark somewhere what'll identify me," he ended, with modest pride.

"Dear me!" squeaked the little old man, greatly impressed. "How interesting! How *very* interesting!"

They had reached the little old gentleman's house. A very prim old lady opened the door.

"You're late, Augustus," she said sternly.

"A most interesting specimen," murmured Augustus deprecatingly. "I found it as I was on the point of returning home and forgot the hour."

The prim lady was looking up and down William.

"Who is this boy?" she said, still more sternly.

"Ah!" said the old gentleman, as if glad to change the subject, "he is a little gipsy."

"Nasty creatures!" put in the lady fiercely.

"But he has told me his story," said Augustus eagerly, peering at William again over the top of his spectacles. "Interesting—most interesting. If you'll just come into my study with me a moment."

The lady pointed to a chair in the hall.

"Sit there, boy," she said to William.

After a few minutes she and the little old gentleman came into the hall again. "Where's this birthmark you speak of?" said the old lady severely.

Without a moment's hesitation, William pointed to a small black mark on his wrist.

The lady looked at it suspiciously.

"My brother will go back with you to the encampment to verify your strange story," she said. "If it is untrue I hope they will be very severe with you. Don't be long, Augustus."

"No, Sophia," said Augustus meekly, setting off with William.

William was rather silent. It was strange how adventures seemed to have a way of getting beyond control.

"I don't remember the peacocks very plain," he said at last.

"Hush!" said the old man, taking out his magnifying glass. He crept up to a tree-trunk. He gazed at it in a rapt silence.

"Most interesting," he said. "I much regret having

left my notebook at home."

"An', of course," said William, "anyone might dream about stachues."

They found that the encampment had gone. There was no mistake about it. There were the smouldering remains of the fire and the marks of the wheels of the caravan. But the encampment had disappeared. They went to the end of the wood, but there were no signs of it along any of the three roads that met there. The little old gentleman was distraught.

"Oh, dear, oh, dear!" he said. "How unfortunate! Do you know where they were going next?"

"No," said William truthfully.

"Oh, dear, oh, dear! What shall we do?"

"Let's go back to your house," said William trustingly. I should think it's about dinner time."

"Well," said Sophia grimly, "you've kidnapped a child from a gipsy encampment, and I hope you're prepared to take the consequences."

"Oh, dear," said the old gentleman, almost in tears. "What a day! And it opened so propitiously. I watched a perfect example of a scavenger beetle at work for nearly half an hour and then—this."

William was watching them with a perfectly expressionless face.

"Never mind," he said. "It doesn't matter what happens to-day. It's extra."

"We must keep the boy," said Augustus, "till we have made inquiries."

"Then he must be washed," said Sophia firmly, "and those dreadful clothes must be fumigated."

William submitted to the humiliating process of being washed by a buxom servant. He noticed, with misgiving, that his birthmark disappeared in the process. He resisted all attempts on the part of the maid-servant at intimate conversation.

"A deaf moot, that's wot I calls 'em," said the maid indignantly, "an' me wastin' my kindness on 'im an' takin' a hinterest in 'im an' 'im treatin' me with scornful silence like. A deaf moot 'e is."

The lady called Sophia had entered, carrying a short, white, beflounced garment.

"This is the only thing I can find about your size, boy," she said. "It's a fancy dress I had made for a niece of mine about your size. Although it has a flimsy appearance, the thing is made on a warm wool lining. My niece was subject to bronchitis. You will not find it cold. You can just wear it while you have dinner, while your clothes are being—er—heated."

A delicious smell was emanating from a saucepan on the fire. William decided to endure anything rather than risk being ejected before that smell materialised.

He meekly submitted to Helbert's garments being taken from him. He meekly submitted to being dressed in the white, beflounced costume. He remembered to take his two paper bags from the pockets of Helbert's knickers and tried, unsuccessfully, to find pockets in the costume he was wearing, and finally sat on them. Then, tastefully arrayed as a Fairy Queen, he sat down at the kitchen table to a large plateful of stew. It was delicious stew. William felt amply rewarded for all the indignities to which he was submitting. The servant sat opposite watching him.

"Is all gipsies deaf moots?" she said sarcastically.

"I'm not an ornery gipsy," said William, without raising his eyes from his plate, or ceasing his appreciative and hearty consumption of Irish stew. "I was stole by the gipsies, I was. I've gotter birthmark somewhere where you can't see it what'll identify me."

"Lor!" said the maid.

"Yes, an' I rec'lect peacocks an' stachues—an'—folks walkin' about in crowns."

"Crikey!" said the maid, filling his plate again with stew.

"Yes," said William, attacking it with undiminished gusto, "an' the suit I was wearin' when they stole me is all embroidered with crowns an' peacocks an'—an'——"

"An' stachues, I suppose," said the servant.

"Yes," said William absently.

"An' you was wearin' silver shoes an' stockings, I suppose."

"Gold," corrected William, scraping his plate clean of the last morsel.

"Lor!" said the maid, setting a large plate of pudding before him. "Now, while you're a-heatin' of that I'll jus' pop round to a friend next door an' bring of 'er in. I shun't like 'er to miss 'earin' you talk—all dressed up, like what you are, too. It's a fair treat, it is."

She went, closing the door cautiously behind her.

William disposed of the pudding and considered the situation. He felt that this part of the adventure had gone quite far enough. He did not wish to wait till the maid returned. He did not wish to wait till Augustus or Sophia had "made inquiries."

He opened the kitchen door. The hall was empty. Sophia and Augustus were upstairs enjoying their after-dinner naps. William tiptoed into the hall and put on one of the coats.

Fortunately, Augustus was a very small man, and the coat was not much too large for William. William gave a sigh of relief as he realised that his humiliating costume was completely hidden. Next he put on one of Augustus's hats.

There was no doubt at all that it was slightly too big.

Then he returned to the kitchen, took his two precious paper packets from the chair, put them into Augustus's coat pockets and crept to the front door. It opened noiselessly. William tiptoed silently and ungracefully down the path to the road.

All was still. The road was empty.

It seemed a suitable moment to assume the disguise. With all the joy and pride of the artist, William donned his precious false beard. Then he began to walk jauntily up the road.

*   *   *

Suddenly he noticed a figure in front of him. It was the figure of a very, very old man, toiling laboriously up the hill, bending over a stick. William, as an artist, never scorned to learn. He found a stick in the ditch and began to creep up the hill with little faltering steps, bending over his stick.

He was thoroughly happy again.

He was not William.

He was not even Helbert.

He was a very old man, with a beard, walking up a hill.

The old man in front of him turned into the work-house gates, which were at the top of the hill. William followed. The old man sat on a bench in a courtyard. William sat beside him. The old man was very short-sighted.

"'Ello, Thomas," he said.

William gave a non-committal grunt. He took out his battered paper bag and handed a few fragments of crumbled cake to the old man. The old man ate them. William, thrilling with joy and pride, gave him some more. He ate them. A man in uniform came out of the door of the workhouse.

"Arternoon, George," he said to the old man.

He looked closely at William as he passed.

Then he came back and looked still more closely at William. Then he said: "'Ere!" and whipped off William's hat. Then he said: "Well, I'm——!!" and whipped off William's beard. Then he said: "I'll be——" and whipped off William's coat.

William stood revealed as the Fairy Queen in the middle of the workhouse courtyard.

The short-sighted old man began to chuckle in a high, quavering voice. "It's a lady out of a circus," he said. "Oh, dear! Oh, dear! It's a lady out of a circus!"

The man in uniform staggered back with one hand to his head.

"Gor' blimey!" he ejaculated. "'Ave I gone mad, or am I a-dreamin' it?"

"It's a lady out of a circus. He! He!" cackled the old man.

But William had gathered up his scattered possessions indignantly and fled, struggling into the coat as he did so. He ran along the road that skirted the work-house, then, finding that he was not pursued, and that the road was empty, adjusted his hat and beard and buttoned his coat.

At a bend in the road there was a wayside seat, already partially occupied by a young couple. William, feeling slightly shaken by the events of the last hour, sat down beside them. He sat there for some minutes, listening idly to their conversation, before he realised with horror who they were. He decided to get up and unostentatiously shuffle away. They did not seem to have noticed him so far. But Miss Flower was demanding a bunch of the catkin palm that grew a little farther down the road. Robert, William's elder brother, with the air of a knight setting off upon a dangerous quest for his ladye, went to get it for her. Miss Flower turned to William.

WILLIAM STOOD REVEALED AS THE FAIRY QUEEN IN THE
MIDDLE OF THE COURTYARD. THE SHORT-SIGHTED OLD MAN
BEGAN TO CHUCKLE. "IT'S A LADY OUT OF A CIRCUS! OH,
DEAR! OH, DEAR!"

"Good afternoon," she said.

William shaded the side of his face from her with his
hand and uttered a sound, which was suggestive of
violent pain or grief, but whose real and only object was
to disguise his natural voice.

Miss Flower moved nearer to him on the seat.

"Are you in trouble?" she said sweetly.

William, at a loss, repeated the sound.

She tried to peer into his face.

"Could—could I help at all?" she said, in a voice whose womanly sympathy was entirely wasted on William.

William covered his face with both his hands and emitted a bellow of rage and desperation.

Robert was returning with the catkins. Miss Flower went to meet him.

"Robert," she said, "have you any money. I've left my purse at home. There's a poor old man here in dreadful trouble."

Robert's sole worldly possessions at that moment were two and sevenpence halfpenny. He gave her half a crown. She handed it to William, and William, keeping his face still covered with one hand, pocketed the half-crown with the other.

THE MAN IN UNIFORM STAGGERED BACK WITH ONE HAND TO HIS HEAD.

"Do speak to him," whispered Miss Flower. "See if you can help him at all. He may be ill."

Robert sat down next to William and cleared his throat nervously.

"Now, my man——" he began, then stopped abruptly, staring at all that could be seen of William's face.

He tore off the hat and beard.

"You little wretch! And whose coat are you wearing, you little idiot?"

He tore open the coat. The sight it revealed was too much for him. He sank back upon the seat with a groan.

Miss Flower sat on the grass by the roadside and laughed till the tears ran down her cheeks.

"Oh, William!" she said. "You are priceless. I'd just love to walk through the village with you like that. Will you come with us, Robert?"

"*No*," said Robert wildly. "At every crisis of my life that boy turns up and always in something ridiculous. He's—he's more like a nightmare than a boy."

*   *   *

William faced a family council consisting of his father and mother, and Robert and Ethel.

William was still attired as a Fairy Queen.

"Well," said William, in a tone of disgust. "You said to-day was extra. I thought it didn't count. I thought nothin' anyone did to-day counted. I thought it was an extra day. An' there's Robert takin' a half-crown off me an' no one seems to mind that. An' Robert tellin' Miss Flower, on the seat, how he'd wanted to live a better life since he met her."

Robert's face went scarlet.

"An' then takin' a half-crown off me," William continued. "I don't call that livin' a better life. *She* gave it me an' *he* took it off me. I don't call that being noble like what he said she made him want to be. I don't——"

"Shut *up*," said Robert desperately. "Shut up and I'll give you the wretched thing back."

"All right," said William, receiving the half-crown.

"What I want to know, William," said Mrs. Brown almost tearfully, "is—where are your clothes?"

William looked down at his airy costume.

"Oh, she took 'em off me an' put this thing on me. She said she wanted to heat 'em up. I dunno why. She took off my green jersey an' my——"

"You weren't wearing a jersey," screamed Mrs. Brown.

William's jaw dropped.

"Oh, *those* clothes! Crumbs! I'd forgotten about those clothes. I—I suppose Helbert's still gottem."

Mr. Brown covered his eyes with his hand.

"Take him away," he groaned. "Take him away! I can't bear the sight of him like that any longer!"

Mrs. Brown took him away.

She returned about half an hour later. William, tired by the events of his extra day, had fallen at once into an undeservedly peaceful slumber.

"It'll take us weeks probably to put whatever he's done to-day right," she said hysterically to her husband. "I do hope you'll be severe with him."

But Mr. Brown, freed from the horrible spectacle of William robed as a Fairy Queen, had given himself up to undisturbed and peaceful enjoyment of the fire and his armchair and evening paper.

"To-morrow," he promised pacifically. "Not to-day. You forget. To-day doesn't count."

"Eavesdropping," burst out Robert suddenly. "Simply eavesdropping. I don't know how he can reconcile that with his conscience."

"Let's all be thankful," said Mr. Brown, "that February 29th only happens every four years."

"Yes, but William doesn't," said Robert gloomily. "William happens all the year round."

Chapter 12

William Enters Politics

When William at the Charity Fair was asked to join a sixpenny raffle for a picture, and shown the prize—a dingy oil painting in an oval gilt frame—his expression registered outrage and disgust.

It was only when his friend Ginger whispered excitedly: "I say, William, las' week my aunt read in the paper about someone what scraped off an ole picture like that an' found a real valuable ole master paintin' underneath an' sold it for more'n a thousand pounds," that he hesitated. An inscrutable expression came upon his freckled face as he stared at the vague head and shoulders of a lightly clad female against a background of vague trees and elaborate columns.

"All right," he said, suddenly holding out the sixpence that represented his sole worldly assets, and receiving Ticket number 33.

"Don't forget it was me what suggested it," said Ginger.

"Yes, an' don't forget it was my sixpence," said William sternly.

William was not usually lucky, but on this occasion the number 33 was drawn, and William, purple with embarrassment, bore off his gloomy-looking trophy. Accompanied by Ginger he took it to the old barn.

They scraped off the head and shoulders of the

mournful and inadequately clothed female, and they scraped off the gloomy trees, and they scraped off the elaborate columns. To their surprise and indignation no priceless old master stood revealed. Being thorough in all they did, they finally scraped away the entire canvas and the back.

"Well," said William, raising himself sternly from the task when nothing scrapable seemed to remain, "an' will you kin'ly tell me where this valu'ble ole master is?"

"Who said definite there *was* a valu'ble ole master?" said Ginger in explanation. "'F you kin'ly remember right p'raps you'll kin'ly remember that I said that an aunt of mine *said* that she *saw* in the paper that *someone'd* scraped away an ole picture an' found a valu'ble ole master. I never said——"

William was arranging the empty oval frame round his neck.

"P'raps now," he interrupted ironically, "you'd like to start scratchin' away the frame, case you find a valu'ble ole master frame underneath."

"Will it hoop?" said Ginger with interest, dropping hostilities for the moment.

They tried to "hoop" it, but found that it was too oval. William tried to wear it as a shield but it would not fit his arm. They tried to make a harp of it by nailing strands of wire across it, but gave up the attempt when William had cut his finger and Ginger had hammered his thumb three times.

William carried it about with him, his disappointment slightly assuaged by the pride of possession, but its size and shape were hampering to a boy of William's active habits, so in the end he carefully hid it behind the door of the old barn which he and his friends generally made their headquarters, and then completely forgot it.

*　　　*　　　*

The village was agog with the excitement of the election. The village did not have a Member of Parliament all to itself—it joined with the neighbouring country town—but one of the two candidates, Mr. Cheytor, the Conservative, lived in the village, so feeling ran high.

William's father took no interest in politics, but William's uncle did.

William's uncle supported the Liberal candidate, Mr. Morrisse. He threw himself whole-heartedly into the cause. He distributed bills, he harangued complete strangers, he addressed imaginary audiences as he walked along the road, he frequently brought one hand down heavily upon the other with the mystic words: "Gentlemen, in the sacred cause of Liberalism——"

William was tremendously interested in him. He listened enraptured to his monologues, quite unabashed by his uncle's irritable refusals to explain them to him. Politically the uncle took no interest in William. William had no vote.

William's uncle was busily preparing to hold a meeting of canvassers for the cause of the great Mr. Morrisse in his dining-room. Mr. Morrisse, a tall, thin gentleman, for some obscure reason very proud of his name, who went through life saying plaintively, "double S E, please," was not going to be there. William's uncle was going to tell the canvassers the main features of the programme with which to dazzle the electors of the neighbourhood.

"I s'pose," said William carelessly, "you don't mind me comin'?"

"You suppose wrong then," said William's uncle. "I most emphatically mind your coming."

"But why?" said William earnestly. "I'm *int'rested*. I'd like to go canvassing too. I know a lot 'bout the

rackshunaries—you know, the ole Conservies—I'd like
to go callin' 'em names, too. I'd like——"

"You may *not* attend the Liberal canvassers' meeting,
William," said William's uncle firmly.

From that moment William's sole aim in life was to
attend the Liberal canvassers' meeting. He and Ginger
discussed ways and means. They made an honest and
determined effort to impart to William an adult
appearance, making a frown with burnt cork, and
adding whiskers of matting which adhered to his cheeks
by means of glue. Optimists though they were, they
were both agreed that the chances of William's
admittance, thus disguised, into the meeting of the
Liberal canvassers was but a faint one.

So William evolved another plan.

* * *

The dining-room in which William's uncle was to hold
his meeting was an old-fashioned room. A hatch, never
used, opened from it on to an old stone passage.

The meeting began.

William's uncle arrived and took his seat at the head
of the table with his back to the hatch. William's uncle
was rather short-sighted and rather deaf. The other
Liberal canvassers filed in and took their places round
the table.

William's uncle bent over his papers. The other
Liberal canvassers were gazing with widening eyes at the
wall behind William's uncle. The hatch slowly opened.
A dirty oval gilt frame appeared, and was by no means
soundly attached to the top of the open hatch. Through
the aperture of the frame appeared a snub-nosed,
freckled, rough-haired boy with a dirty face and a
forbidding expression.

William didn't read sensational fiction for nothing. In

"The Sign of Death," which he had finished by the light
of a candle at 11.30 the previous evening, Rupert the
Sinister, the international spy, had watched a meeting of
masked secret service agents by the means of concealing
himself in a hidden chamber in the wall, cutting out the

MR. MOFFATT MET WILLIAM'S STONY STARE. THE OTHER
HELPERS WERE STARING BLANKLY AT THE WALL.

eye of a portrait and applying his own eye to the hole.
William had determined to make the best of slightly less
favourable circumstances.

There was no hidden chamber, but there was a hatch;
there was no portrait, but there was the useless frame for

"DON'T YOU THINK THAT POINT IS VERY IMPORTANT?" ASKED
WILLIAM'S UNCLE.

which William had bartered his precious sixpence. He still felt bitter at the thought.

William felt, not unreasonably, that the sudden appearance in the dining-room of a new and mysterious portrait of a boy might cause his uncle to make closer investigations, so he waited till his uncle had taken his seat before he hung himself.

Ever optimistic, he thought that the other Liberal canvassers would be too busy arranging their places to notice his gradual and unobtrusive appearance in his frame. With vivid memories of the illustration in "The Sign of Death," he was firmly convinced that to the casual observer he looked like a portrait of a boy hanging on the wall.

In this he was entirely deceived. He looked merely what he was—a snub-nosed, freckled, rough-haired boy hanging up an old empty frame in the hatch and then crouching on the hatch and glaring morosely through the frame.

William's uncle opened the meeting:

". . . and we must emphasise the consequent drop in the price of bread. Don't you think that point is very important, Mr. Moffat?"

Mr. Moffat, a thin, pale youth with a large nose and a naturally startled expression, answered as in a trance, his mouth open, his strained eyes fixed upon William.

"Er—very important."

"Very—we can't over-emphasise it," said William's uncle.

Mr. Moffat put up a trembling hand as if to loosen his collar. He wondered if the others saw it too.

"Over-emphasise it," he repeated, in a trembling voice.

Then he met William's stony stare and looked away hastily, drawing his handkerchief across his brow.

"I think we can safely say," said William's uncle, "that if the Government we desire is returned the average loaf will be three-halfpence cheaper."

He looked round at his helpers. Not one was taking notes. Not one was making a suggestion. All were staring blankly at the wall behind him.

Extraordinary what stupid fellows seemed to take up this work—that chap with the large nose looked nothing more or less than tipsy!

"Here are some pamphlets that we should take round with us . . ."

He spread them out on the table. William was interested. He could not see them properly from where he was. He leant forward through his frame. He could just see the words, "Peace and Prosperity . . ." He leant forward further. He leant forward too far. Accidentally attaching his frame round his neck on his way he descended heavily from the hatch. There was only one thing to do to soften his fall. He did it. He clutched at his uncle's neck as he descended. A confused medley consisting of William, his uncle, the frame and his uncle's chair rolled to the floor where they continued to struggle wildly.

"Oh, my *goodness*," squealed the young man with the large nose hysterically.

Somehow in the mêlée that ensued, William managed to preserve his frame. He arrived home breathless and dishevelled but still carrying his frame. He was beginning to experience a feeling almost akin to affection for this companion in adversity.

"What's the matter?" said William's father sternly. "What have you been doing?"

"Me?" said William in a voice of astonishment. "Me?"

"Yes, you," said his father. "You come in here like a

tornado, half dressed, with your hair like a neglected lawn——"

William hastily smoothed back his halo of stubby hair and fastened his collar.

"Oh, *that*," he said lightly. "I've only jus' been out—walking an' things."

Mrs. Brown looked up from her darning.

"I think you'd better go and brush your hair and wash your face and put on a clean collar, William," she suggested mildly.

"Yes, Mother," agreed William without enthusiasm. "Father, did you know that the Libr'als are goin' to make bread an' everything cheaper an'—an' prosperity an' all that?"

"I did not," said Mr. Brown dryly from behind his paper.

"I'd give it a good brushing," said his wife.

"If there weren't no ole rackshunary Conservy here," said William, "I s'pose there wouldn't be no reason why the Lib'ral shouldn't get in?"

"As far as I can disentangle your negatives," said Mr. Brown, "your supposition is correct."

"I simply can't *think* why it always stands up so straight," said Mrs. Brown plaintively.

"Well, then, why don't they *stop* 'em?" said William indignantly. "Why do they *let* the old Conserves come in an' spoil things an' keep bread up—why don't they *stop* 'em—why——"

Mr. Brown uttered a hollow groan.

"William," said he grimly. "Go—and—brush—your—hair."

"All right," he said. "I'm jus' goin'."

*   *   *

Mr. Cheytor, the Conservative candidate, had

addressed a crowded meeting and was returning wearily to his home.

He opened the door with his latchkey and put out the hall light. The maids had gone to bed. Then he went upstairs to his bedroom. He opened the door. From behind the door rushed a small whirlwind. A rough bullet-like head charged him in the region of his abdomen. Mr. Cheytor sat down suddenly. A strange figure dressed in pyjamas, and over those a dressing-gown, and over that an overcoat, stood sternly in front of him.

"You've gotter *stop* it," said an indignant voice. "You've gotter stop it an' let the Lib'rals get in—you've gotter stop——"

Mr. Cheytor stood up and squared at William. William, who fancied himself as a boxer, flew to the attack. The Conservative candidate was evidently a boxer of no mean ability, but he lowered his form to suit William's. He parried William's wild onsets, he occasionally got a very gentle one in on William. They moved rapidly about the room, in a silence broken only by William's snortings. Finally Mr. Cheytor fell over the hearthrug and William fell over Mr. Cheytor. They sat up on the floor in front of the fire and looked at each other.

"Now," said Mr. Cheytor soothingly. "Let's talk about it. What's it all about?"

"They're goin' to make bread cheaper—the Lib'rals are," panted William, "an' you're tryin' to stoppem an' you——"

"Ah," said Mr. Cheytor, "but we're going to make it cheaper, too."

William gasped.

"You?" he said. "The Rackshunaries? But—if you're both tryin' to make bread cheaper why're you fightin' each other?"

"You know," said Mr. Cheytor, "I wouldn't bother about politics if I were you. They're very confusing mentally. Suppose you tell me how you got here."

"I got out of my window and climbed along our wall to the road," said William simply, "and then I got on to your wall and climbed along it into your window."

"Now you're here," said Mr. Cheytor, "we may as well celebrate. Do you like roasted chestnuts?"

"Um-m-m-m-m-m," said William.

"Well, I've got a bag of chestnuts downstairs—we can roast them at the fire. I'll get them. By the way, suppose your people find you've gone?"

"My uncle may've come to see my father by now, so I don't mind not being at home jus' now."

Mr. Cheytor accepted this explanation.

"I'll go down for the chestnuts then," he said.

* * *

Fortune was kind to William. His uncle was very busy and thought he would put off the laying of his complaint before William's father till the next week. The next week he was still more busy. Encountering William unexpectedly in the street he was struck by William's (hastily assumed) expression of wistful sadness, and decided that the whole thing may have been a misunderstanding. So the complaint was never laid.

Moreover, no one had discovered William's absence from his bedroom. William came down to breakfast the next day with a distinct feeling of fear, but one glance at his preoccupied family relieved him. He sat down at his place with that air of meekness which in him always betrayed an uneasy conscience. His father looked up.

"Good morning, William," he said. "Care to see the paper this morning? I suppose with your new zeal for politics——"

"Oh, politics!" said William contemptuously. "I've given 'em up. They're so—so," frowning he searched in his memory for the phrase, "They're so—confusing ment'ly."

His father looked at him.

"Your vocabulary is improving," he said.

"You mean my hair?" said William with a gloomy smile. "Mother's been scrubbin' it back with water same as what she said."

William walked along the village street with Ginger. Their progress was slow. They stopped in front of each shop window and subjected the contents to a long and careful scrutiny.

"There's nothin' *there* I'd buy 'f I'd got a thousand pounds."

"Oh, isn't there? Well, I jus' wonder. How much 've you got, anyway?"

"Nothin'. How much have you?"

"Nothin'."

"Well," said William, continuing a discussion which their inspection of the General Stores had interrupted, "I'd rather be a Pirate than a Red Indian—sailin' the seas an' finding hidden treasure——"

"I don't quite see," said Ginger with heavy sarcasm, "what's to prevent a Red Indian finding hidden treasure if there's any to find."

"Well," said William heatedly, "you show me a single tale where a Red Indian finds a hidden treasure. That's all I ask you to do. Jus' show me a *single* tale where a——"

"We're not talkin' about tales. There's things that happen outside tales. I suppose everything in the world that can happen isn't in tales. 'Sides, think of the war-whoops. A Pirate's not got a war-whoop."

"Well, if you think——"

They stopped to examine the contents of the next shop window. It was a second-hand shop. In the window was a medley of old iron, old books, broken photograph frames and dirty china.

"An' there's nothin' *there* I'd wanter buy if I'd got a thousand pounds," said William sternly. "It makes me almost glad I've *got* no money. It mus' be mad'ning to have a lot of money an' never see anything in a shop window you'd want to buy."

Suddenly Ginger pointed excitedly to a small card propped up in a corner of the window, "Objects purchased for Cash."

"William," gasped Ginger. "The frame!"

A look of set purpose came into William's freckled face. "You stay here," he whispered quickly, "an' see they don't take that card out of the window, an' I'll fetch the frame."

Panting, he reappeared with the frame a few minutes later. Ginger's presence had evidently prevented the disappearance of the card. An old man with a bald head and two pairs of spectacles examined the frame in silence, and in silence handed William half a crown. William and Ginger staggered out of the shop.

"Half a crown!" gasped William excitedly. "Crumbs!"

"I hope," said Ginger, "you'll remember who suggested you buying that frame."

"An' I *hope*," said William, "that you'll remember whose sixpence bought it."

This verbal fencing was merely a form. It was a matter of course that William should share his half a crown with Ginger. The next shop was a pastry-cook's. It was the type of pastry-cook's that William's mother would have designated as "common." On a large dish in the middle of the window was a pile of sickly-looking yellow pastries full of sickly-looking yellow butter cream. William pressed his nose against the glass and his eyes widened.

"I say," he said, "only a penny each. Come on in."

They sat at a small marble-topped table, between them a heaped plate of the nightmare pastries, and ate in silent enjoyment. The plate slowly emptied. William ordered more. As he finished his sixth he looked up. His uncle was passing the window talking excitedly to Mr. Morrisse's agent. Across the street a man was pasting up a poster, "Vote for Cheytor." William regarded both with equal contempt. He took up his seventh penny horror and bit it rapturously.

"Fancy," he said scornfully, "fancy people worryin' about what *bread* costs."

Chapter 13

William Makes a Night of it

William had disliked Mr. Bennison from the moment he appeared, although Mr. Bennison treated him with most conscientious kindness. William disliked the way Mr. Bennison's hair grew and the way his teeth grew and the way his ears grew, and he disliked most of all his agreeable manner to William himself. He was not used to agreeable manners from adults, and he distrusted them.

Mr. Bennison was a bachelor and wrote books on the training of children. He believed that children should be led, not driven, that their little hearts should be won by kindness, that their innocent curiosity should always be promptly satisfied. He believed that children trailed clouds of glory. He knew very few. He certainly did not know William.

Mr. Bennison had met Ethel, William's sister, while she was staying with an aunt. Ethel possessed blue eyes and a riot of auburn hair of which William was ashamed. He considered that red hair was quite inconsistent with beauty. He found that most young men who met Ethel did not share that opinion.

Although Mr. Bennison had reached the mature age

of forty without having found any passion to supersede his passion for educational theories, he experienced a distinct quickening of his middle-aged heart at the sight of Ethel with her forget-me-not eyes and copper locks. William never could understand what men "saw in" Ethel. William considered her interfering and bad-tempered and stingy, and everything that an ideal sister should not be. Yet there was no doubt that adult males "saw something" in her.

And William had the wisdom to make capital out of this distorted idea of beauty whenever he could.

William was in that state of bankruptcy which occurred regularly in the middle of each week. He was never given enough pocket money to last from Saturday to Saturday. That was one of his great grievances against life. And just now there were some pressing calls on his purse.

It was Ginger, William's boon companion, who had seen the tops in the shop window and realised suddenly that the top season was upon them once more. The next day, almost the whole school was equipped with tops.

Only William and Ginger seemed topless. To William, a born leader, the position was intolerable. It was Wednesday. The thought of waiting till Saturday was not for one moment to be entertained. Money must somehow or other be raised in the interval.

Tops of a kind could be bought for sixpence, but the really superior tops—the tops which befitted the age and dignity of William and Ginger—cost one shilling, and William and Ginger, never daunted by difficulties, determined to raise the sum by the next day.

"We mus' get a shilling each," said William, with his expression of grim and fixed determination, "an' we'll buy 'em to-morrow."

"Well, you know what my folks are like," said Ginger despondently. "You know what it's like tryin' to get money out of 'em. '*Save* your pocket money,' they say. If they'd *give* me enough I'd be able to save. What's sixpence? Could anyone save sixpence? It's gone in a day— sixpence is. An' they say 'save'," he ended bitterly.

"Well," said William "all I can say is that no one's folks can be stingier than mine, and that if I can get a shilling——"

"Yes, but you've not got it yet, have you?" taunted Ginger.

"No," said William confidently, "but you wait till to-morrow!"

*   *   *

William had spoken confidently, but he felt far from confident. He knew by experience the difficulty of extorting money from his family. He had tried pathos, resentment, indignation, pleading, and all had failed on every occasion. He was generally obliged to have recourse to finesse. He only hoped that on this occasion Fate would provide circumstances on which he could exercise his finesse.

He entered the drawing-room, and it was then that he first saw Mr. Bennison. It was then that he took a violent and definite dislike to Mr. Bennison, yet he had a wild hope that he might be a profitable source of tips. With a mental vision of the tops before his eyes he assumed an expression of virtue and innocence.

"So this," said Mr. Bennison, with a genial smile, "is the little brother."

William's expression of virtue melted into a scowl. William was eleven years old. He objected to being called a "little" anything.

"I heard there was a little brother," went on the visitor, perpetrating the supreme mistake of laying his hand upon William's tousled head. "'Will' is the name, is it not? 'Willie' for short, I presume? Ha! Ha!"

Mrs. Brown, noting fearfully the expression upon her son's face, interposed.

"We call him William," she said rather hastily.

"I call him 'Willie'—for short," smiled Mr. Bennison, patting William's unruly locks.

Mr. Bennison laboured under the delusion that he "got on with" children. It was well for his peace of mind that William's face was at that moment hidden from him. It was only the thoughts of the top which might be the outcome of all that made William endure the indignity.

"And I have brought a present for Willie-for-short," went on Mr. Bennison humorously.

William's heart rose. It might be a top. It might be something he could exchange for a top. Best of all, it might be money.

But Mr. Bennison took a book out of his pocket and handed it to William.

The book was called "A Child's Encyclopædia of Knowledge."

Mrs. Brown, who could see William's face, went rather pale.

"Say 'Thank you,' William dear," she said nervously, then, hastily covering William's murmured thanks,

"How very kind of you, Mr. Bennison. How very kind. He'll be most interested. I'm sure he will, won't you, William, dear? Er—I'm sure he will."

William freed himself from Mr. Bennison's hand, and went towards the door.

"You will remember," went on Mr. Bennison pleasantly, "that in my 'Early Training of the Young' I lay down the rule that every present given to a child should tend to his or her mental development. I do not believe in giving a child presents of money before he or she is sixteen. No really wise faculty of choice is developed before then. I expect you remember that in my 'Parents' Help,' I said——"

William crept quietly from the room.

*　　*　　*

He went first of all to Ethel's bedroom.

She was reading a novel in an arm-chair.

"Go away!" she said to William.

In the midst of his preoccupation William found time to wonder again what people "saw in" her. Well, if they only *knew* her as well as he did . . . But the all-important question was the question of tops.

"Ethel," he said in a tone of brotherly sweetness and Christian forgiveness, "have you got any tops left? You must have had tops when you were young. I wonder if you'd like to give 'em to me 'f you've got any left, an' I'll use 'em up for you."

"Well, I've not," snapped Ethel, "so go away."

William turned to the door, then turned back as if struck by a sudden thought.

"D'you remember, Ethel," he said, "that I took a spider out of your hair for you las' summer? I wondered 'f you'd care to lend me a shilling jus' till my next pocket money——"

"You *put* it in my hair first," said Ethel indignantly, "and I jolly well won't, and I wish you'd go away."

William looked at her coldly.

"*How* people can say you're 'tractive——" he said. "Well, all I can say is wait till they *know* you, an' that man downstairs coming jus' 'cause of you an' worrin' folks' lives out an' strokin' their heads an' givin' 'em books—well, you'd think he'd be ashamed, an' you'd think you'd be ashamed, too!"

Ethel had flushed.

"You needn't think I want him," she said. "I should think I'm the only person who can grumble about *him* being here. I have to stay up here all the afternoon just because I can't bear the nonsense he talks when I'm down."

"How long's he staying?" said William.

"Oh, a week," said Ethel viciously. "He said he was motoring in the neighbourhood, and mother asked him to stay a week. She likes him. He's got three cars and a lot of money, and he can talk the hind leg off a donkey, and she likes him. All I can say," bitterly, "is that I'm going to have a nice week!"

"What about a shilling?" said William, returning to the more important subject. "Look here, 'f you lend me a shilling now I'll give you a shillin *an'* a penny when I get my pocket money on Saturday. I'll not forget. A shillin *an'* a penny for a shilling. I should think you'd call it a bargain."

"Well, I wouldn't," said Ethel, "and I wish you'd go—*away.*"

"I don't call you very gen'rous, Ethel," said William loftily.

"No, and I'm not likely to be generous or feel generous with that man in the house," said Ethel.

William was silent. He was silent for quite a long

time. William's silences generally meant something.

"S'pose," he said at last, "s'pose he went to-morrow, would you feel generous, then?"

"I would," said Ethel recklessly. "I'd feel it quite up to two shillings in that case. But he won't go. Don't you think it! And-will-you-go *away?*"

William went, rather to her surprise, without demur.

He walked very slowly downstairs. His brow was knit in thought.

Mr. Bennison was still talking to Mrs. Brown in the drawing-room.

"Oh, yes, that is one of my very firmest tenets. I have laid stress on that in all my books. The child's curiosity must always be appeased. No matter at what awkward time the child propounds the question, he or she must be answered courteously and fully. Curiosity must be appeased the moment it appears. If a child came to me in the middle of the night for knowledge," he laughed uproariously at his joke, "I trust I should give it to the best of my ability, fully, and—er—as I said . . . Ah, here is our little Willie-for-short."

Still holding his "Child's Encyclopædia of Knowledge," William turned and quickly left the room.

*   *   *

Mr. Bennison had had a good dinner and a pleasant talk with Ethel before he came to bed.

The talk had been chiefly on his side, but he preferred it that way. He was thinking how pleasant would be a life in which he could talk continuously to Ethel, while he looked at her blue eyes and auburn hair.

He wrote a chapter of his new book, heading it "Common Mistakes in the Treatment of Children."

He insisted in that chapter that children should be treated with reverence and respect. He laid down his favourite rule: "A child's curiosity must be immediately satisfied when and where it appears, irrespective of inconvenience to the adult."

Then he got into bed.

The bed was warm and comfortable and he was drifting blissfully into a dreamless sleep when the door opened and William, clad in pyjamas and carrying the "Child's Encyclopædia of Knowledge," appeared.

" 'Scuse me disturbin' you," said William politely, "but it says in this book what you kindly gave me somethin' about Socrates" (William pronounced it in two syllables "So-crates") "an' I thought p'raps you wun't mind explaining to me what they are. I dunno what So-crates are."

Mr. Bennison was on the whole rather pleased. In all his books he had insisted that if the child came for knowledge at midnight the child's curiosity must be satisfied then and there, and he was glad of an opportunity of living up to his ideals. He dragged his mind back from the rosy mists of sleep and endeavoured to satisfy William's thirst for knowledge.

He talked long and earnestly about Socrates, his life and teaching and his place in history. William listened with an expressionless face.

Whenever the other seemed inclined to draw his remarks to a close William would gently interpose a question which would set his eloquence going again at full flow. But Mr. Bennison's eyes began to droop and his eloquence began to languish. He looked at his watch. It was 12.30.

"I think that's all, my boy," he said with quite a passable attempt at bluff, hearty kindness in his voice.

"You haven't quite 'splained to me——" began William.

"I've told you all I know," said Mr. Bennison irritably.

William, still clasping his book, went quietly from the room.

Mr. Bennison turned over and began to go to sleep. It took a little time to get over the interruption, but soon a delicious drowsiness began to steal over him.

Going—going——

William entered the room again, still carrying his "Child's Encyclopædia of Knowledge."

"It says in this book what you kindly gave me," he said earnestly, "all about Compound Interest, but I don't quite understand——"

William was very clever at not understanding Compound Interest. He had an excellent repertoire of intelligent questions about Compound Interest. At school he could, for a consideration, "play" the Mathematics master on Compound Interest for an entire lesson while his friends amused themselves in their own way in the desks behind.

Mr. Bennison's eloquence was somewhat lacking in lucidity and inspiration this time, but he struggled gallantly to clear the mists of William's ignorance. At times the earnestness of William's expression touched him. At times he distrusted it. At no time did it suggest those clouds of glory that he liked to associate with children. By 1.30 he had talked about Compound Interest till he was hoarse.

"I don't think there's anything else I can tell you," he said with an air of irritation which he vainly endeavoured to hide. "Er—shut the door after you. It's very draughty when you leave it open—er—dear boy."

William, with the utmost docility, went out of the room.

*   *   *

Mr. Bennison turned over and tried to go to sleep. It did not seem so easy to go to sleep this time. There is something about explaining Compound Interest to the young and ignorant that is very stimulating to the brain.

He tried to count sheep going through a stile and they persisted in turning into the figures of a Compound Interest sum. He tried to call back the picture of domestic happiness with which the sight of William's sister had inspired him earlier in the evening, and always the vision of William's earnest, inscrutable countenance rose to spoil it.

Sheep—one—two—three—four—five——

The door opened, and William appeared with the open book once more in his hand.

"In this book what you kindly gave me," he began, "it tells about the stars an' the Lion an' that, an' I can't find the Lion from the window, though the stars are out. I wondered 'f you'd kindly let me look through yours."

Sheep and stile vanished abruptly. After a short silence pregnant with unspoken words, Mr. Bennison sat

up in bed. He looked very
weary as he stared at
William, but he was dog-
gedly determined to act up
to his ideals.

"I don't think you can
see the Lion from this side
of the house, my boy," he
said, in what he imagined
was a kind tone of voice,
"it must be right on the opposite side of the house."

"Then we could see it
from my window," said
William brightly and
guilelessly, "if you'd kin'ly
come an' help me find it."

Mr. Bennison said
nothing for a few seconds.
He was counting forty to
himself. It was a proceed-
ing to ensure self-control
taught him by his mother
in early youth. It had never
failed him yet, though it
nearly did on this occa-
sion. Then he followed
William across the landing
to his room.

THE DOOR OPENED AND
WILLIAM APPEARED FOR
THE THIRD TIME. "IN THIS
BOOK WHAT YOU KINDLY
GAVE ME," HE BEGAN, "IT
TELLS ABOUT THE STARS."

William was not content with the Lion. He insisted on
finding all the other constellations mentioned in the
book. At 2.30 Mr. Bennison staggered back to his
bedroom. He did not go to bed at once. He took out the
chapter he had written early in the evening and crossed
out the words, "A child's curiosity must be immediately

MR. BENNISON SAT UP IN BED. HE LOOKED VERY WEARY AS HE
STARED AT WILLIAM.

satisfied when and where it appears, irrespective of
inconvenience to the adult.''

He decided to cut out all similar sentiments in the next
editions of all his books.

Then he got into bed. Sleep at last—blissful, drowsy,
soul-satisfying sleep.

"Mr. Bennison—*Mr. Bennison*—in this book what
you kindly gave me there's some kind of puzzles—
''telligence' tests' it calls 'em, an' I can't do 'em. I
wondered if you'd kindly help me——''

"Well, I won't," said Mr. Bennison. "Go away. Go
away, I tell you."

"There's only a page of 'em," said William.

"Go away," roared Mr. Bennison, drawing the clothes over his head. "I tell you I won't—I *won't*——"

William quietly went away.

Now Mr. Bennison was a conscientious man. Left alone in the silence of the night all desire for sleep deserted him. He was horrified at his own depravity. He had deliberately broken his own rule. He had been false to his ideals.

He had refused to satisfy the curiosity of the young when and where it appeared. A child had come to him for help in the middle of the night and he had refused him or her. The child, moreover, might repeat the story. It might get about. People might hold it up against him.

After wrestling with his conscience for half an hour he arose and sought William in his room. At four o'clock he was still trying to solve the intelligence tests for William. William stood by wearing that expression that Mr. Bennison was beginning to dislike intensely.

At 4.15 Mr. Bennison, looking wild and dishevelled, returned to his room. But he was a broken man. He struggled no longer against Fate. Five o'clock found him explaining to William exactly why Charles I had been put to death.

Six o'clock found him trying to fathom the meaning of "plunger" and "inductance" and "slider" and various other words that occurred in the chapter on Wireless. It fortunately never occurred to him that they were all terms with which William was perfectly familiar.

As he held his head and tried to think from what Greek or Latin words the terms might have been derived, he missed the flicker that occasionally upset the perfect repose of William's features.

At seven o'clock he felt really ill and went downstairs to try to find a whisky-and-soda. It was not William's fault that he fell over the knitting on which Mrs. Brown had been engaged the evening before, and which had slipped from her chair on to the floor. His frenzied efforts to disentangle his feet entangled them still further.

At last, with teeth bared in rage and wearing the air of a Samson throwing off his enemies, he tore wildly at the wool, and scattering bits of this material and unravelled socks about him, he strode forward to the sideboard. He could not find a whisky-and-soda. After upsetting a cruet in the sideboard cupboard he went guiltily back to his bedroom.

His bed looked tidier than he imagined he had left it, and very inviting. Perhaps he might get just half an hour's sleep before he got up . . . He flung himself on to the bed. His feet met with an unexpected resistance half-way down the bed, bringing his knees sharp up to his chin. The bed was wrong. The bed was all wrong. The bed was all very wrong.

For a few seconds Mr. Bennison forgot the traditions of self-restraint and moderation of language on which he had been reared. William, standing in the doorway, listened with interest.

"I hope you don't mind me tryin' 'f I could do it," he said. "I dunno why it's called an apple-pie bed, do you? It doesn't say nothing about it in this book what you kindly gave me."

Mr. Bennison flung himself upon William with a roar. William dodged lightly on to the landing. Mr. Bennison followed and collided heavily with a housemaid who was carrying a tray of early morning tea.

* * *

William came down to breakfast. He entered the dining-room slowly and cautiously. Only his father and mother were there. His mother was talking to his father.

"He wouldn't even stay for breakfast," she was saying. "He said his letter called him back to town on most urgent business. I didn't like his manner at all."

"Oh?" said her husband from behind his paper, without much interest.

"No, I thought it rather ungracious, and he looked queer."

"Oh?" said her husband, turning to the financial columns.

"Yes—wild and hollow-eyed and that sort of thing. I've wondered since whether perhaps he takes drugs. One reads of such things, you know, and he certainly looked queer. I'm glad he's gone."

William went up to Ethel's bedroom. Ethel was gloomily putting the finishing touches to her auburn hair.

"He's gone, Ethel," he said in a conspiratorial whisper, "gone for good."

Ethel's countenance brightened.

"Sure?" she said.

"Sure," he said. "Now what 'bout that two shillings?"

She looked at him with sudden suspicion.

"Have you——?" she began.

"Me?" broke in William indignantly. "Why, I din' know he'd gone till I got down to breakfast."

"All right," said Ethel carelessly. "If he's really and truly gone, I'll give you half a crown."

* * *

William, on his way to school, met Ginger at the end of the lane.

"I've tried 'em all," said Ginger despondently, "an' none of 'em'll give me a penny."

William with a flourish brought out his half a crown.

"This'll do for both of us," he said with a lordly air.

"Crumbs!" said Ginger, with respect and admiration in his voice. "Who d'you get that out of?"

"Well, a man came to stay at our house——" began William.

Ginger's respect and admiration vanished.

"Oh, a *visitor!*" he said disparagingly. "'S easy enough to get money out of a visitor."

"'F you think *this* was easy," began William with deep feeling, then stopped.

It was a long story and already retreating into the limbo of the past. He could not sully the golden present by a lengthy repetition of it. It had been jolly hard work while it lasted, but now it was over and done with. It belonged to the past. The present included a breathless run into the village, leaping backwards and forwards across the ditches, a race down the village streets and TOPS—glorious tops—superior shilling-each tops with sixpence over.

He uttered his shrill, discordant war-whoop.

"Come on," he shouted, "'fore they're all sold out. Race you to the end of the road!"

Chapter 14

A Dress Rehearsal

It was Saturday, but despite that glorious fact, William, standing at the dining-room window and surveying the world at large, could not for the moment think of anything to do.

From the window he saw the figure of his father, who sat peacefully on the lawn reading a newspaper. William was not fond of his own society. He liked company of any sort. He went out to the lawn and stood by his father's chair.

"You've not got much hair right on the top of your head, father," he said pleasantly and conversationally.

There was no answer.

"I said you'd not got much hair on the top of your head," repeated William in a louder tone.

"I heard you," said his father coldly.

"Oh," said William, sitting down on the ground. There was silence for a minute, then William said in friendly tones:

"I only said it again 'cause I thought you didn't hear the first time. I thought you'd have said, 'Oh,' or 'Yes,' or 'No,' or something if you'd heard."

There was no answer, and again after a long silence, William spoke.

"I didn't mind you not sayin' 'Oh', or 'Yes,' or 'No',"

he said, "only that was what made me say it again, 'cause with you not sayin' it I thought you'd not heard."

Mr. Brown arose and moved his chair several feet away. William, on whom hints were wasted, followed.

"I was readin' a tale yesterday," he said, "about a man wot's legs got bit off by sharks——"

Mr. Brown groaned.

"William," he said politely, "pray don't let me keep you from your friends."

"Oh, no, that's quite all right," said William. "Well—p'raps Ginger is lookin' for me. Well, I'll finish about the man an' the sharks after tea. You'll be here then, won't you?"

"Please, don't trouble," said Mr. Brown with sarcasm that was entirely lost on his son.

"Oh, it's not a trouble," said William as he strolled off, "I like talkin' to people."

*　　*　　*

Ginger was strolling disconsolately down the road looking for William. His face brightened when he saw William in the distance.

"Hello, William."

"Hello, Ginger."

In accordance with their usual ceremonial greeting, they punched each other and wrestled with each other till they rolled on to the ground. Then they began to walk along the road together.

"I've not got to stop with you long," said Ginger gloomily; "my mother's got an ole Sale of Work in her garden, an' she wants me to help."

"Huh!" said William scornfully, "*you* helpin' at a Sale of Work! *You*. Huh!"

"She's goin' to give me five shillings," went on Ginger coldly.

William slightly modified his tone. "Well, I never said you can't help, did I?" he said in a more friendly voice.

"She said I needn't go for about half an hour. Wot'll we do? Dig for hidden treasure?"

Two months ago William and his friends had been fired with the idea of digging for hidden treasure. From various books they had read ("Ralph the Reckless," "Hunted to Death," "The Quest of Captain Terrible," etc.), they had gathered that the earth is chockful of buried treasure if only one takes the trouble to dig deep enough.

They had resolved to dig every inch of their native village, collect all the treasure they found, and with it buy a desert island on which they proposed to spend the rest of their lives unhampered by parents and school-masters.

They had decided to begin with the uncultivated part of Ginger's back garden, and to buy further land for excavation with the treasure they found in the back garden.

Their schemes were not narrow. They had decided to purchase and to pull down all the houses in the village as their treasure grew and more and more land was required for digging.

But they had dug unsuccessfully for two months in Ginger's back garden and were beginning to lose heart. They had not realised that digging was such hard work, or that ten feet square of perfectly good land would yield so little treasure. Conscientiously they carried on the search, but it had lost its first fine careless rapture, and they were glad of any excuse for avoiding it.

"Dig in your back garden with all those Sale of Work people messin' about interruptin' and gettin' in the way?" said William sternly. "Not much!"

"All right," said Ginger, relieved. "I only *s'gested* it. Well, shall we hunt for smugglers?"

* * *

There was a cave in the hillside just beneath the road, and though the village in which William and Ginger lived was more than a hundred miles inland, William and Ginger were ever hopeful of finding a smuggler or, at any rate, traces of a smuggler, in the cave. They searched it carefully every day.

As William said, " 'S only likely the reely cunnin' ones wouldn't stay sittin' in their caves by the sea all the time. They'd know folks'd be on the look out for 'em there. They'd bring their things here where no one'd expect 'em. Why, with a fine cave like this there's *sure* to be smugglers."

When tired of hunting for smugglers, or traces of smugglers, they adopted the characters of smugglers themselves, and carried their treasure (consisting of stones) up the hillside to conceal it in the cave, or fled for their lives to the cave with imaginary soldiers in pursuit. From the cover of the cave, Bill, the smuggler, often covered the entire hillside with the dead bodies of soldiers. In these frays the gallant smugglers never received even the slightest scratch.

With ever fresh hope they searched the cave again. Ginger found a stone that he said had not been there yesterday, and must have been left as a kind of signal, but William said that he distinctly recognised it as having been there yesterday, and the matter dropped.

After a brief and indecisive discussion as to how they should spend the five shillings that Ginger's mother had said she would give him, they occupied themselves in crawling laboriously on their stomachs in and out of the cave so as to be unperceived by the soldiers who were on the watch above and below.

At last, Ginger, moved not so much by his conscience as by fears of forfeiting his five shillings, set off sadly homewards, and William set off along the road in the opposite direction.

He walked slowly, his hands in his pockets, dragging his shoes in the dust in a manner which his mother frequently informed him brought the toes through in no time.

*   *   *

When he came to the school he stopped, attracted by the noise that came through the open window of the schoolroom. They were preparing for a dress rehearsal of the "Pageant of Ancient Britain," which was to be performed the next month. William, who was not in the cast, looked with interest through the window. Ancient Britons in various stages of skins and woad and grease-paint stood about the room or leap-frogged over each other's backs or wrestled with each other in corners. William espied a particular enemy at the other end of the room. He put his head through the window.

"Hello, Monkey Brand," he called in his strident, devastating voice.

Miss Carter, mistress of the Second Form, raised herself wearily from arranging the skin of an infant Ancient Briton.

"I wish you wouldn't," she began testily, then, her voice sinking into hopelessness, "Oh, it's William Brown."

William, ignoring her, put his fingers to his lips and, still gazing belligerently at his enemy, emitted a deafening whistle. Miss Carter put her hands to her ears.

"*William!*" she said irritably.

William wiped his mouth with the back of his hand.

"Beg pardon," he said mechanically and without feeling, as he withdrew his head and prepared to retire.

"Oh, one minute, William. What are you doing just now?"

William inserted his untidy head in the window again.

"Me?" he said. "Nothin'. Jus' nothin'."

"Well, I wish you'd come and be an Ancient Briton just for the dress rehearsal—it won't be long, but so many of them can't come this afternoon, and it's so difficult to arrange how they're to stand with only three-quarters of them there. You needn't be madé up, but just put this skin on."

She held up a small skin carelessly in her hand. William looked round the room with his sternest and most disapproving scowl.

"Have I gotter come in with all those boys all over the place an' change with all those boys botherin' me all the time so's I don't know wot I'm doin' an'——"

Miss Carter was in a bad temper. She threw the skin irritably at William through the window.

"Oh, change where you like," she snapped, "if you'll be back here in five minutes."

William took the skin eagerly.

"Oh, yes, I will," he promised.

Then he rolled up the skin and stuffed it under his arm. It instantly changed into a bale of precious but vague contraband material.

Glancing sternly round for soldiers, William crept cautiously and silently down to his cave. There he drew a sigh of relief, placed his gun in a corner and changed into the skin. Once clad in the skin, his ordinary clothes became the precious but vague contraband material. He crept to the entrance, glanced furtively around, then wrapped his clothes into a bundle and looked around for some place of concealment. On the ground at the further end of the cave was a large piece of paper in which he and Ginger had once brought their lunch.

Still with many furtive glances around, he wrapped up his clothes, and concealed the bundle on a shelf of rock in the corner of the cave. Then he took up his gun, shot two soldiers who were just creeping towards the entrance of the cave, walked to the doorway, shot again at a crowd of soldiers who fled in panic terror at his approach. Then, resplendent in his skin and drunk with heroism and triumph, he swaggered up the hillside and into the school.

*   *   *

As an Ancient Briton, he was not an unqualified success, and more than once Miss Carter regretted her casual invitation. William considered the rehearsal as disappointing as the rehearsal considered him—just standin' about an' singin' an' talkin'—no fightin' nor shoutin' or nothin'. He was glad he *wasn't* a Nanshunt Briton, if that's all the poor things could do.

However, at last it was over, and he crept again furtively down the hillside to his private dressing-room. Ginger was standing near the cave entrance.

"What've you been *doin'* all this time?' he began; then, as his gaze took in William's costume, his mouth opened.

"Crumbs!" he said.

"I'm a Nanshunt Briton," said William, airily.

"They jus' wanted me to go an' be a Nanshunt Briton up at the school an'——"

"Well," interrupted Ginger excitedly, "while you've been away I've *found* 'em at last."

"What?" said William.

"Smugglers!" said Ginger excitedly. "Smugglers' things."

"Golly!" said William, equally thrilled. "Where?"

"In the cave—when I came to look for you, an' I cun't find you, an' I looked round the cave again, an' I found 'em."

A sudden fear chilled William's enthusiasm.

"What were they?"

"Clothes an' things. I thought I wun't look at 'em prop'ly till you came. They were wrapped up in that ole paper we brought our food in last week."

The Ancient Briton looked at him sternly and accusingly.

"Yes—well, they were my clothes wot I'd changed out of, that's what they were. You're jus' a bit too clever takin' people's clothes for smugglers' things. Anyway, I'm jus' gettin' cold with only a skin on, so jus' please give me those smugglers' things, so's I can put 'em on."

Ginger's jaw dropped.

"I—I took 'em home. I didn't want to leave 'em about here case someone else found 'em. I hid 'em behind a tree in our garden."

The Ancient Briton's gaze became still more stern.

"Well, p'raps you'd kin'ly gettem for me out of your garden 'fore I die of cold, dressed in only a skin. I should think the Anshunt Britons all died of cold if they felt like wot I feel like. You're jus' a bit too clever with other people's smugglers' things: an' s'pose Miss Carter comes down for her skin an' wot d'you think I'll look like then, dressed in nothin'?"

"All right," said Ginger. "I'll gettem. I won't be a minute. If you will leave your clothes all about the cave lookin' *exactly* like smugglers' things——"

He was gone, and William sat shivering in a corner of the cave, dressed in his Ancient Briton costume. The glamour of the cave was gone. William felt that he definitely disliked smugglers. The only people he disliked more than he disliked smugglers were Ancient Britons, for whom he now felt a profound scorn and loathing.

In about ten minutes time Ginger returned. He was empty handed, and there was a look of consternation on his face.

"William," he said meekly, "I'm awfully sorry. It's been sold. They thought it was meant for the rummage stall, an' they've took it an' sold it."

William was speechless with indignation.

"Well," he said at last, "you've gone an' sold all my clothes—an' now what do you thin's goin' to happen to me? That's jus' wot I'd like to know, 'f you don' mind tellin' me. Wot's goin' to happen to me? P'raps as you've sold all my clothes, you'll kin'ly tell me wot's goin' to happen to me, gettin' colder an' colder. P'raps you'd like me to freeze to death. How'm I goin' to get home, an' if I don't get home how'm I goin' to get anythin' to eat, and if I don't get anythin' to eat, how'm I goin' to live? I'm dyin' of cold now. Well, I only hope you'll be sorry then—then, when prob'ly you'll be bein' hung for murderin' me." William returned to earth from his flights of fancy. "Well, now, p'raps you'll kin'ly get my clothes back."

"How can I?" said Ginger, with the air of one goaded beyond endurance.

"Well, you can go an' find out who bought 'em, I suppose—only you needn't tell 'em whose they was."

Again Ginger departed, and again the Ancient Briton sat shivering and gazing sternly and accusingly around the cave.

After a short interval Ginger appeared again, breathless with running.

"WELL," SAID WILLIAM STERNLY, "YOU'VE GONE AND SOLD
ALL MY CLOTHES—AN' NOW WHAT DO YOU THINK'S GOING TO
HAPPEN TO ME? HOW'M I GOIN' TO GET HOME?"

"Mr. Groves bought it, William, from Wayside Cottage. I dunno how I'm to get 'em back, though, William."

William sighed.

"I'd better come with you," he said wearily. "'Sides, I shall prob'ly get froze into a glacier or something if I stay in here any more."

The Ancient Briton gazed furtively around from the cave door, without that bravado and swagger generally displayed by Bill the Smuggler. The coast was clear. The two boys crept out.

"When I get to the road, I'll crawl on my stomach in the ditch like as if I were a smuggler, then no one'll see me."

Ginger walked dejectedly along the road, while the Ancient Briton made a slow and very conspicuous progress in the ditch beside him—ejaculating irascibly as he went:

"Well, I've jus' *done* with smugglers *an'* with Anshunt Britons. I'll never look at another smuggler *or* a Nanshunt Briton while I live—'n if you hadn't been so jolly *clever* runnin' off with other people's clothes, an' *sellin'* 'em, I shouldn't be crawlin' along *an'* scratchin' myself, *an'* cuttin' myself, an' eatin' mud. Now," in a voice of pure wonder, "how did Anshunt Britons get about? I don't know—all shiverin' with cold an' scratchin' themselves *an'* cuttin' themselves——"

Wayside Cottage was, fortunately for the Ancient Briton, on the outskirts of the village. The front door was conveniently open. There was a small garden in front, and a longer garden behind, with a little corrugated iron building at the end.

"Come on," said William. "Let's go an' get 'em back."

"Are you goin' to ask him for 'em?" said Ginger.

"No, I'm *not*. I don't want everyone in this village talking about it," said William sternly. "I jus' want to get 'em back quietly an' put 'em on' an' no one know anything about it. I don't want anyone *talkin'* about it."

No one was about. They gazed at the stairs from the open doorway. "They'll be upstairs," said William in a hoarse whisper, "clothes are always upstairs. Now, come *very* quietly. *Creep* upstairs."

Ginger followed him loyally, fearfully, reluctantly, and they went upstairs. Every time Ginger hit a stair rod, or made a stair creak, William turned round with a stern and resonant "Sh!" At last they reached the landing. William cautiously opened the door and peeped within. It was a bedroom, and it was empty.

"Come on," whispered William, with the cheerfulness of the born optimist. "They're sure to be here."

They entered and closed the door.

"Now," said William, "we'll look in all the drawers and then we'll look in the wardrobe."

They began to open the drawers one by one. Suddenly Ginger said "Hush!"

There was the sound of footsteps coming up the stairs. They drew nearer the door.

"Crumbs!" gasped William. "Under the bed—quickly!"

As they disappeared under the bed the door opened

and a little old gentleman came in. He looked round at the open drawers and frowned.

"How curious!" he said as he shut them; "how very curious!"

Then he hummed to himself, straightened his collar at the glass, took a few little dancing steps round the room, and then stood irresolute, his hand on his chin.

"Now what did I come up for?" he said. "What did I come up for? Ah! A handkerchief."

All might have been well had not the Ancient Briton at this moment succumbed to the united effects of cold and dust, and emitted a resounding sneeze.

"Bless my soul!" said the old gentleman. "Bless my——"

He dived beneath the bed, and, seizing hold of William's bare and muddy foot, he pulled. But William had firm hold of the further leg of the bed, and the old gentleman, exerting his utmost strength, only succeeded in pulling the bed across the room with William still firmly attached to it. But this treatment infuriated William.

"'F you'd kin'ly stop draggin' me about on my stomach——" he began, then emerged, stern and dusty, and arranging his skimpy and dishevelled skin.

"You—you—you *thief!*" said the old man.

"I'm not a thief," said William, "I'm a Nan-shunt——"

But the old man made a dash at him and William dodged and fled out of the doorway. Ginger was already half-way downstairs. The old man was delayed, first by the door, which William banged in his face, and secondly, by the fact that he slipped on the top stair and rolled down to the bottom.

There he sat up, looked for his spectacles, found

them, adjusted them and gazed round the hall, still seated on the hall mat. The two boys were nowhere to be seen. Muttering "Dear! Dear!" and "Bless my soul! Let me see, what was it I wanted?—Ah, a handkerchief!" the old man began to ascend the stairs.

* * *

But William and Ginger had not gone out of the front door. A group of Ginger's mother's friends could be plainly seen passing the little gateway, and in panic William and Ginger had dashed out of the back door into the little garden, and into the corrugated iron building. A lady, dressed in an artist's smock, a paint brush in her hand, looked up from an easel.

"Please don't come in quite so roughly," she said disapprovingly. "I don't like rough little boys." She looked William up and down, and her disapproval seemed to deepen. "Well," she said stiffly, "it doesn't seem to me *quite* the costume. I should have thought the Vicar—— However, you'd better stay now you've come. Is the other little boy your friend? He must sit down quite quietly and not disturb us. You may just look at the picture first for a treat." Bewildered, but ready to oblige her, William wandered round and looked at it. It seemed to consist of a chaos of snow and polar bears.

"It's to be called 'The Frozen North'," she said proudly. "Now you must stand in the attitude of one drawing a sleigh—so—no, the expression more *gentle*, please. I must say I do *not* care for the costume, but the Vicar must know——"

"I'm a Nanshunt——" began William, then decided to take the line of least resistance and be the Frozen North. The lady painted in silence for some time, occasionally looking at William's rather mangy skin, and saying disapprovingly: "No, I must *say*—I do *not*—but, of course, the Vicar——"

Just as the charm of novelty was disappearing from the procedure, and he was devising means of escape, another lady came in.

"Busy, dear?" she said, then she adjusted her lorgnettes, and she, too, looked disapprovingly at William.

"My dear!" she said. "Isn't that rather—— Well, of course, I know you artists are—well, Bohemian and all that, but——"

WILLIAM DASHED FOR THE DOORWAY, UPSETTING THE OLD GENTLEMAN ON HIS WAY.

The artist looked worried.

"My dear," she said, "I showed the Vicar the picture yesterday, and he said that he had a child's Eskimo costume, and he'd find a boy to fit in and send it round for a model. But—I'd an idea that the Esquimos dressed more—er—*completely* than that, hadn't you?"

"I'm a Nanshunt——" began William, and stopped again.

"You remember Mrs. Parks asking for money to buy clothes for her boy?" went on the artist as she painted. "Well, I got John to go to that Sale of Work this

THE OLD GENTLEMAN LANDED ON TOP OF THE CANVAS AND
SAT THERE MURMURING, "OH, DEAR! OH, DEAR!"

afternoon and get a suit from the rummage stall, and he
got quite a good suit, and I've just sent it round to her.
Do stand *still*, little boy—— You know, dear, I wish I
felt happier about this—er—costume. Yet I feel I ought
not to criticise and even in my mind, anything the dear
Vicar——"

"Well, I'll be quite frank," said the visitor. "I don't
care for it—and I do think that artists can't be too
careful—any suggestion of the nude is so—well, don't
you agree with me? I'm *surprised* at the Vicar."

The artist held out half a crown to William.

"You may go," she said coldly. "Take the costume
back to the Vicar, and I *don't* think I shall require you
again."

At that moment the little old man came in. He started
as his eye fell on William and Ginger.

"The *thief!*" he said excitedly. "The *thief!* Catch him,
catch him, *catch* him!"

William dashed to the doorway, upsetting the old man
and a wet canvas on his way. The old man landed on top
of the canvas and sat there murmuring, "Oh, dear, oh
dear, what a day!" and looking for his glasses.

The visitor pursued the two of them half-heartedly to
the gate, and then returned to help in the work of
separating the old gentleman from the wet canvas.

*   *   *

William and Ginger sat in a neighbouring ditch and
looked at each other breathlessly.

"Parks," said Ginger, "that's the shop at the end of
the village."

"Yes," said William, "an' I'm jus' about sick of
crawlin' in ditches, an' what's wrong with it I'd like to
know," he went on, looking down indignantly at his limp

skin, "it's all right—not as clothes—but as a kind of
dress-up thing it's all right—as good as that ole
pinnyfore *she* was wearing, an' I jolly nearly said so—an'
'thief,' too. Well, I wun't go *inside* that house again, not
if—not if—not if they *asked* me—Anyway," his expression softened, "anyway, I got half a crown," his
expression grew bitter once more, "half a crown, an' not
even a pocket to put it in. Come on to Parks'."

William returned to the ditch. They only passed a
little girl and her small brother.

"Look, Algy," said the little girl, "look at 'im. 'E's a
loony an' the other's 'is keeper. 'E thinks 'e's a frog,
prob'ly, an' that's why 'e goes in ditches, an' doesn't
wear no clothes."

William straightened himself.

"I'm a Nanshunt——" he began, but at sight of his red
and muddy face, surmounted by its crest of muddy hair,
the little girl fled screaming.

"Come on, Algy, 'e'll get yer an' eat yer if yer
don't——"

Algy's screams reinforced hers, and William disconsolately returned to the ditch as the screams, still lusty,
faded into the distance.

"I'm jus' getting a bit sick of this," muttered the
Ancient Briton.

*   *   *

They reached Parks'. William lay concealed behind
the hedge, and Ginger wandered round the shop,
reconnoitring.

"Go in!" goaded William, in a hoarse whisper from
the hedge. "Go in an' gettem. Say you'll fetch a
policeman—*make* 'em give 'em you—*fight* 'em—*take*
'em—*you* lettem go—I can't stand this much longer. I'm

cold an' I'm wet. I feel as if I'd been a Nanshunt Briton for years an' years—hurry up——— Are-you-goin'-to-get-my-*clothes?*"

"Oh, shut *up!*" said Ginger miserably. "I'm doin' all I can."

"Doin' all you can, are you? Well, you're not doin' much but walkin' round an' round the shop. D'you think 'f you go on walkin' round and round the shop my clothes'll come out of themselves—come *walkin'* out to you? 'Cause if you think that——"

"Shut *up*." . . . .

At this moment a small boy walked out of the shop.

"Hallo!" said Ginger, with a fatuous smile of friendship.

"Hallo!" said the boy, ungraciously.

Ginger moistened his lips and repeated the fatuous smile.

"Have you got any new clothes to-day?"

The boy gave a fairly good imitation of the fatuous smile.

"No," he said, "have you? Don't go spoilin' your fice for me. It's bee-utiful, but don't waste it on me."

Then, whistling, he prepared to walk away from Ginger down the road. Desperately Ginger stopped him.

"I'll—I'll—I'll give you," he swallowed, then, with an effort, made the nobler offer. "I'll give you five shillings if——"

"Yus?" said the boy suddenly, "if——?"

"If you'll give me those clothes the lady wot paints sent you to-day."

"Gimme the five shillings then."

"I won't give you the money till you give me the clothes."

"Oh, won't you? Well, I won't give you the clothes till

you give me the money."

They stared hostilely at each other.

"Get my clothes," said the irate voice from the ditch. "Punch him—do anythin' to him. Get—my—clothes."

The boy looked round with interest into the ditch.

"Look at 'im!" he shrieked mirthfully. "Look at 'im. *Na*kid—jus' dressed in a muff—Oh! look at 'im."

William arose with murder in his face. Ginger hastily pressed five shillings into the boy's hand.

"Gettem quick," he said.

The boy retreated to the shop and closed the door except for a small crack. Through that crack he shouted, "We din' want no narsty, mangy, mouldy, cast-off clothes from no one. We gived 'em to Johnsons up the village."

Then he banged the door.

William, in fury, kicked the door, and a crowd of small boys collected. William, perceiving them, fled through the hedge and into the field. The small boys followed, uttering derisive cries.

"*Look* at 'im—*Look* at 'im—'e's a cannibal—he's got no clothes—'e' out of a circus—'e's balmy—'e's wearin' 'is mother's fur."

William turned on them in fury.

"I'm a Nanshunt——" he began, rushing upon them; and they fled in panic.

William and Ginger sat down behind a haystack.

"Well, you're very clever at gettin' back my clothes, aren't you?" said William with heavy sarcasm.

"I'm gettin' jus' about sick of your clothes," said Ginger gloomily.

"Sick of 'em?" echoed William. "I only wish I'd gotten to be sick of. I'm jus' about sick of not havin' 'em an' walkin' about on prickles an' stones and scratchin' myself an' shiverin' with cold. That boy'd jus' better wait till I *get* my clothes an' then——" His eyes gleamed darkly with visions of future vengeance.

"Well," he turned to Ginger, "an' wot we goin' to do now?"

"Dunno," said Ginger despondently.

"Well, where's Johnsons'?"

"Mrs. Johnson's my aunt's charwoman," said Ginger, wearily. "I know where she lives."

William rose with a determined air.

"Come on," he said.

"If we don't gettem this time," said Ginger, as they started on their furtive journey. "I'm going home."

"Oh, are you," said William sternly. "Well, then, you're goin' in this Anshunt Briton thing an' I'm goin' in your clothes. You lost my clothes an' if you can't gettem back you can give me yours, that's fair, isn't it?"

"Oh, shut *up*," said Ginger, in the tone of one who has suffered all that it is possible to suffer and can suffer no more. "It's that five shillings that I keep thinkin' of—*five shillin's*—an' all for nothin'."

"An' callin' my clothes mouldy," said William, with equal indignation. "*My* clothes mouldy."

"She lives here," said Ginger.

From the shelter of a hedge they watched the house.

"You'd better go an' gettem then," said William unfeelingly.

"*How?*" said Ginger.

"Well, you sold 'em."

"I *didn't* sell 'em."

"Sh! Look!"

The door of the Johnsons' home was opening. A small boy came out.

"He's dressed in my clothes," said William excitedly. "*Gettem—Gettim*—my clothes." His eyes brightened, and into his face came a radiant look as of one beholding some dear friend after a long absence. "My clothes."

Ginger advanced to the small boy and smiled his anxious, fatuous, mirthless smile.

"Like to come an' play with me?" he said.

"Yeth, pleth," said the boy, returning the friendly smile.

"Well, you can come with me," said Ginger ingratiatingly.

He followed Ginger through the stile, and gave a shout of derision when he saw William crouching behind the hedge. "Oh! *Look* at 'im," he said, "dressed up funny."

A masterly plan had come into William's head. He led the party to the next field, to the disused barn which, in their normal happy life that now seemed to him so far away, served as castle or pirate ship.

"Now," he said, "we're goin' to play at soldiers, an' you come an' say you wanter join the army——"

"But I don't," said the small boy solemnly. "That would be a thtory."

"Never mind," said William patiently. "You must pretend you want to join the army. Then you must take off your clothes and leave 'em with me, and this boy will pretend to be the doctor; an' he'll tell you if you're strong enough, you know; he'll look at your lungs and things and then—and then—well, that's all. Now I'll give you the half-crown jus' for a present if you play it prop'ly."

"All right," said the boy brightly, beginning to take off his coat.

"You've got bad lungs, an' a bad heart, an' bad legs, an' bad arms, an' bad ears, an' a bad head," said the doctor, "an' I'm *afraid* you can't be a soldier."

"All right," said the boy brightly. "Don' wanter be. Now I'll put on my clothes."

He came out to the back of the barn, where he had left his clothes, and burst into a howl.

"Oooo—oo—oo—'e's tooken my clothes—tooken my clothes—'e's tooken my clothes. Ma! *Ma! Ma!* 'E's tooken my clothes."

His shirt fluttering in the wind, he went howling down the road.

Ginger went to the ditch whence William's gesticulating arms could be seen.

"Quick! William, quick!" gasped Ginger.

William arose, holding his Ancient Briton costume in his hand. He was clothed in a tweed suit—a very very small tweed suit—the waistcoat would not button across him and the sleeve came only a little way below his elbow.

"William!" gasped Ginger. "It's not yours."

William's face was pale with horror.

"It looked like mine," he said in a sepulchral voice, "but it's not mine."

A babel of voices arose.

"Where are they, lovey?"

"Boo—hoo—they've tooken my clothes."

"Wait till I gettem, that's all."

"Never mind, darlin'. Ma'll learn 'em."

With grim despair they saw what seemed to them an army of women running up the hill, and with them a howling boy in a fluttering shirt. One of the women carried a broom.

"*Run*, William!" gasped Ginger.

William flung his skin into the ditch and ran. Though his suit was so tight that he could only progress in little leaps and bounds, he progressed with remarkable speed.

* * *

At last, exhausted and breathless, he walked round to the side entrance of his home and stood in the hall. He could hear his mother's voice from the drawing room.

"Miss Carter's been ringing up all the afternoon," she was saying, "she seems to think that William took away one of the costumes after the rehearsal. I told her that I was sure William wouldn't do such a thing."

"My dear," in his father's voice, "you do make the most rash statements."

William entered slowly. His father and mother and sister turned and stared at him in silence.

"William!" gasped his mother. "What *are* you wearing?"

William made a desperate effort to carry off the situation.

"You know—everyone says how fast I'm growin'—I keep growin' out of my things——"

"Mother!" screamed Ethel, from the window, "there's a lot of awful women coming through the gate and an awful little boy in a shirt!"

*   *   *

William was brushed and combed and dressed in his best suit. His week-day suit had been, with great trouble and at great expense, brought back from Mrs. Johnson, and taken from the person of her eldest son, and was now being disinfected from any possible germ which might have infested the person of her eldest son.

Mrs. Johnson and her indignant younger son had been, with great difficulty and also at great expense, soothed and appeased.

William had eaten the bread and water considered, in the circumstances, a suitable meal for the prodigal son, with that inward fury, but with that outward appearance of intense enjoyment that he always fondly imagined made his family feel foolish.

He was not to leave the garden again that day. He was to go to bed an hour before his usual time, but that left him now half an hour to dispose of in the garden.

Through the window William could see his father reclining in a deck-chair and reading the evening paper. William considered that his father had that evening shown himself conspicuously lacking in tact and sympathy and generosity, but William did not bear malice, and he knew that such qualities are not to be expected in grown-ups. Moreover, his father was the only human being within sight, and William felt disinclined for active pursuits. He went out to his father and sat down on the grass in front of him.

"Oh, about that man wot had his legs bit off by a shark, father, wot I promised to tell you about—well, it begins when he starts out in the Ship of Mystery——"

William's father tried to continue to read his paper. Finding it impossible, he folded it up.

"One minute, William, how long is there before you go to bed?"

"Only about half an hour," said William reproachfully. "But I can tell you quite a lot in that time, an' I can go on to-morrow if I don't finish it. You'll *like* it—Ginger'n me liked it awfully. Well, starts off in the Ship of Mystery, an' why it's called the Ship of Mystery is because every night there's ghostly moanin's an' rattlin's of chains, an' one day the man wot the tale's about went down to get something he'd forgot in the middle of the night, an' he saw a norful figure dressed in a long black cloak, with gleamin' eyes, and jus' as he was runnin' away it put out a norful skinny hand, an' said in a norful voice——"

William's father looked wildly round for escape, and saw none.

Nemesis had overtaken him. With a groan he gave himself up for lost, and William, already thrilled to his very soul by his story, the memories of his exciting day already dim, pursued his ruthless recital.